MAGAZINE

Tin House

Volume 19, Number 4

"I think communication is so firsbern."

—STEVE MARTIN

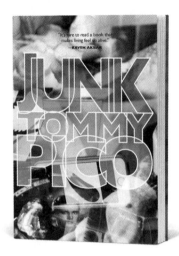

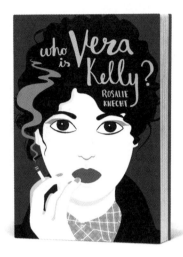

JUNK
poetry by Tommy Pico

Building on *IRL* and *Nature Poem*, Tommy Pico's *Junk* is a book-length break up poem that explores the experience of loss and erasure, both personal and cultural.

"*Junk* is a true American odyssey, complete with a reluctant hero who defies all odds to survive. Repulsed by the trashiness of empire, the violence of occupation, this book nonetheless searches in earnest for real tenderness, a romance that isn't corny. . . . This is poetry of the highest order, on the level of a pop song, with the crystalline visions of a seer. I consumed it greedily, repeatedly, and am forever changed because of it."

—JENNY ZHANG

WHO IS VERA KELLY?
by Rosalie Knecht

A Most Anticipated Book of 2018 at the *Huffington Post*, *Book Riot*, *Bustle*, *Autostraddle*, and more, *Who Is Vera Kelly?* introduces an original, wry, and whip-smart female spy for the twenty-first century.

"Sardonic, intelligent, and thrillingly original, Rosalie Knecht has not only revitalized the female spy novel with her feisty, indeterminable heroine, she's also joyfully queered it. I loved this book and I loved Vera. Read this book right now!"

—COURTNEY MAUM

Available May 2018

Available June 2018

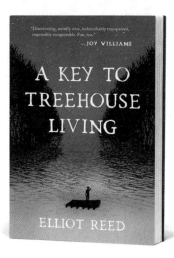

THE SEAS
by Samantha Hunt
Introduction by Maggie Nelson

With the inventive brilliance and psychological insight that have earned her international acclaim, Samantha Hunt pulls readers into an undertow of impossible love and intoxication, blurring the lines between reality and fairy tale, hope and delusion, sanity and madness.

"I read *The Seas* when it first came out and was scalded by its beauty. It took me back to how I felt as a kid, when you're newly falling in love with literature, newly shocked by its capacity to cast a spell—you know the feeling, when you turn the last page of a novel that you've burrowed into and has burrowed into you, and suddenly find that the book has become more than a book, it's become a talisman, something precious. A little scary, a little holy."

—MAGGIE NELSON

A KEY TO TREEHOUSE LIVING
by Elliot Reed

For fans of Mark Haddon, Tony Earley, and Jonathan Safran Foer, an epic tale of boyhood from an unforgettable new voice.

"Disorienting, weirdly wise, indescribably transparent, impossibly recognizable.
Fun, too."

—JOY WILLIAMS

"Powered in part by longing and a need to make odd associations add up, this very appealing novel employs jelly beans and gypsies, tree forts and rafts, and a character known as El Hondero to trace the odd conjuring that this narrator brings us in on. A memorable debut."

—AMY HEMPEL

Available July 2018   **Available September 2018**

Tin House
MAGAZINE

EDITOR IN CHIEF / PUBLISHER
Win McCormack

EDITOR	Rob Spillman
DEPUTY PUBLISHER	Holly MacArthur
ART DIRECTOR	Diane Chonette
MANAGING EDITOR	Cheston Knapp
EXECUTIVE EDITOR	Michelle Wildgen
POETRY EDITOR	Camille T. Dungy
EDITOR-AT-LARGE	Elissa Schappell
PARIS EDITOR	Heather Hartley
ASSOCIATE EDITOR	Emma Komlos-Hrobsky
ASSISTANT EDITOR	Thomas Ross
COPY EDITOR	Meg Storey
SENIOR DESIGNER	Jakob Vala

CONTRIBUTING EDITORS: Dorothy Allison, Steve Almond, Aimee Bender, Charles D'Ambrosio, Natalie Diaz, Anthony Doerr, Nick Flynn, Matthea Harvey, Jeanne McCulloch, Rick Moody, Maggie Nelson, Whitney Otto, D. A. Powell, Jon Raymond, Helen Schulman, Jim Shepard, Karen Shepard

INTERNS: Enma Elias, Jake Bartman, Libby DeBunce, Alexandra Frankland, Cathryn Rose, Meritt Salathe, Kelsey Stoneberger

READERS: Leslie Marie Aguilar, William Clifford, April Darcy, Selin Gökçesu, Todd Gray, Lisa Grgas, Carol Keeley, Louise Wareham Leonard, Su-Yee Lin, Maria Lioutaia, Alyssa Persons, Sean Quinn, Lauren Roberts, Gordon Smith, Jennifer Taylor, J. R. Toriseva, Charlotte Wyatt

Ursula K. Le Guin wrote in her esteemed 1969 novel, *The Left Hand of Darkness*, "I talk about the gods, I am an atheist. But I am an artist too, and therefore a liar. Distrust everything I say. I am telling the truth." And what a fierce truth our Portland neighbor told, right up until her journey's end. Whenever we had the great fortune to publish her, we would take page proofs up the hill to her house, where she would chuckle at our foolishness over tea. In this issue we present a last, long short story, "Pity and Shame," which is filled with her trademark inventiveness and dark humor. I imagine she would be happy with the company in these pages, the other six short stories along with the three essays, all written by women. The passed torch burns bright in the hands of Catherine Lacey, who, in her story "The Grand Claremont Hotel," concocts an infinitely pleasing luxury hotel. You can also see the fiery connection in emerging writer Abbey Mei Otis, whose fiercely imagined story "Rich People" will be included in her debut collection, out this summer from our friends at Small Beer Press, which is helmed by Kelly Link and her husband, Gavin Grant, whose daughter is named for Le Guin. In her essay "Recipe for Mystery," Elissa Schappell divines the magic of Chartreuse, a botanical liqueur made by Carthusian monks in silence and secrecy (the formula of one-hundred-plus herbs has been locked away for centuries). The liqueur was originally formulated in the eighteenth century as the "Elixir of Long Life," but one wouldn't be surprised if it had been conjured by the mind and pen of Le Guin. She will be deeply missed. Luckily for all of us, her words and spirit live on.

CONTENTS

ISSUE #76 / SUMMER READING

Fiction

Poetry

Nonfiction

Lost & Found

Blithe Spirit

Pity and Shame

Ursula K. Le Guin

Hard lot! encompass'd with a thousand dangers;
Weary, faint, trembling with a thousand terrors;
I'm called, if vanquish'd, to receive a sentence
Worse than Abiram's.

      —W. COWPER, "Lines Written During a Period of Insanity"

At first Mr. Cowper just lay there like a heap of bedclothes, laundry for the wash. His face was so blank it was like it was erased off a slate. Doc Mac said he was concussed and he'd probably get over it and probably survive, awful as his injuries looked. Mostly there was nothing to do for him but get him to drink water or beef broth when he'd take it, and use the bedpan.

It had been Pete's idea to take in a lodger, but then he'd complained all week about living in two rooms instead of four. Now that the man was there all the time and she had to be up nights to look after him, Pete was ugly about it, spite of the good pay Doc got her for nursing. He stayed out a lot. When he was home he'd come in and watch what she did like he was suspicious. One night she was giving the bedpan, he kept crowding her till she finally had to say, "I need some room, Petey." He pressed closer. Annoyed with him, she said, "Guess you've seen one of them before."

"Some bigger'n that," he said.

"Come on, honey, I'm on the job."

"Not much of a job."

"More than you got," she said.

After she said it she realised it had another meaning than the one she'd meant, and felt her face get red. She didn't know how Pete took it, but either way it was unkind.

"Yeah, what the hell, I'm going," he said. And he went.

. . .

"I could use a hand with this," Doc Mac said. "Where's Pete at?"

"I can do that," she said. He let her show him she could keep the hold he needed while he adjusted the splint.

"Radius is back in line, we'll get that scaphoid tucked back where it belongs," Doc said. "It'll take a while."

She liked how he said "we." He was a tough thin man like a dried-out leather whip, but he always spoke pleasantly. She didn't know what some of the words he used meant, but she could figure it out, or if she asked, he'd answer. It was not an arrangement she was used to, but she liked it.

. . .

"How did the night go?"

"He was awful restless. Hurting. He hollered some."

"Coming to, I hope. Feeling what happened to him."

"I wish I could do more for him."

"Get some breakfast for yourself. Sounds like you had a long night."

> He was a tough thin man like a dried-out leather whip, but he always spoke pleasantly.

"I don't mind," she said, not knowing why she said it, but it was true.

"God intended you for a nurse, Mrs. Tonely."

She watched him washing and salving places where the rocks had torn up Mr. Cowper like he'd been dragged by a runaway horse.

"My name isn't Tonely," she said. "I'm Rae Brown."

He nodded, working away. "That don't change what I said about God's intentions."

Embarrassed all round, she tried to explain. "Well, my aunt Bess was sick for a long time after an operation, and I was looking after her. And my stepdad had these carbuncles I had to learn to treat."

He nodded again. "Just what I said. —Look there. No infection. So far . . . But you get time off to eat, you know."

"I will," she said.

He was a kind man. She wished she could tell him about last night. It had disturbed her. Mr. Cowper had been quiet for a while, so she fell asleep in the chair, and then she woke because somebody was calling out. The voice was strange, like it came from a long ways off, out in the woods or in the hills, somewhere else. It was a name he was calling, Cleo, Cleo. His voice wasn't loud, but pleading, like he was saying, please come, please come, but not really hoping for it. A heartbroken voice in the darkness. The night was silent, getting on towards morning, everything finally quiet at the saloon. She was nearly asleep again when he called out once more in that soft desolate voice, "Cleo!" This time a rooster answered him from across town with a little bugle call broken off short. She got up from the chair and went over to the bed and put her hand on his sweaty hair, whispering, "It's all right, it'll be all right," wanting to comfort that sorrow that came from far away and maybe long ago while he lay here a stranger among strangers. Things were so hard. And no way to talk about them.

· · ·

A bad thought came to her as she drowsed in the old rump-sprung armchair. Where did Mr. Cowper keep his money?

Pete hadn't earned anything since the Bronco Saloon let him go last March. She'd kept the money from her cleaning for Mr. Bingham and the church, and then the two weeks' advance rent from Mr. Cowper, in a Twinings tea tin. When she needed some cash for groceries she found it had all had gone with Pete. It wasn't a big surprise, but it was a hollow feeling. She told herself Mr. Bingham wouldn't put her out of the house so long as she could pay the rent or work it out, and now she had good pay for boarding Mr. Cowper and nursing him.

That night, though, a bad thought came to her as she drowsed in the old rump-sprung armchair near the bed. Where did Mr. Cowper keep his money?

She couldn't worry about it then, in the middle of the night. But she did. Next day as soon as she'd got him looked after she went into the other room of the two he'd sub-rented from her and Petey two weeks ago and looked around. She felt like a criminal, but she looked into his coat pockets, and at the pocketbook she found there, which had twelve dollars in it. She checked the little chest of drawers where he'd put his shirts and stuff. There was nothing else of his in the room but some books and papers on the worktable, and under the table the little humpback trunk that was all his luggage.

He'd locked it, but there was a trunk key lying out on the table with what had been in his pockets when he went up to the mine. She had to look.

Down at the bottom of the trunk she found a billfold with more than two hundred dollars in it in paper and three fifty-dollar gold pieces. Relieved, she shut it all up quick, shoved it back under the table, and wondered what to do with the key. She went out and hid it behind the paper-wasp nest in the outhouse. The wasps were long gone, but it didn't seem like a place Pete, if he came back, or anybody would go sticking their hand in. Let alone if they knew about the black widow. She only wished she didn't, but she'd seen it twice.

．　．　．

She'd said truly that she didn't mind doing this job. She had minded nursing Roy's boils because he was a hateful man, but caring for Aunt Bessie had been a job she loved. The only trouble had been that Bess was a heavy woman and when she first came home from the hospital, Rae at thirteen couldn't even help her to turn over. Rae was a lot stronger now than she'd been then, and Mr. Cowper wasn't a big man. Doc Mac showed her how to change the sheets. And there really wasn't much to do for him. She wasn't lonely or bored. She was grateful for the silence. The house had felt small and cramped when it was full of Pete's big body and deep voice, and his friends that sat around with their hats on, smoking cigars and always talking. Now the quiet spread out in it, and her soul spread out in the quiet.

Some blue jays were yelling cheerfully at each other outside. The window was full of the gold August light. She sat thinking about things.

She thought a good deal about opening Mr. Cowper's trunk. She'd hardly known him in the short time he'd been there; Pete had shown him the rooms. They'd all signed the agreement Mr. Bingham insisted on, and shaken hands. He had a pleasant manner, but good morning and good evening was about it. He had been gone all day at his work with the mine company, and had boarded at Mrs. Metcalf's. It felt bad to go through his things, with him there in the next room knowing nothing about it, and she knowing nothing about him. She had needed to be sure his money was there, but she kept remembering when she looked for it and the memory troubled her. It was very clear; she could see the tray of the little trunk with papers and letters in it and some socks and handkerchiefs. She had lifted out the tray. Under it were some winter clothes and a dress shirt and coat and shoes, and under them a photograph in a cardboard frame of a dignified lady in 1870s dress, a small unframed blurry photograph of a little girl who looked unhappy, and a couple of books. He'd set his work books out on his worktable. The two in the trunk were *Little Dorrit* by Charles Dickens, and *Poems* by William Cowper. His billfold was between the books. She was careful to replace the photographs on the cover of *Poems.*

That was a puzzle. His name was William Cowper. He said it Cooper, but he wrote it that way, like "cowboy." She wondered why. Had he written that book? It was none of her business. She had had no business looking at his books anyhow. The trunk was locked now and the key was in the outhouse with the black widow.

. . .

Well into the shaft, almost past the daylight, he'd heard the framing creak loudly and thought that would be how a sailing ship would creak in a storm. He remembered that. He had set down his lantern to make another note. Looking up, he saw the weak glimmer on the rough pine beams. And that was it. That was all.

It came and went.

So did the ceiling of a room, slices of daylight, voices, blue jays squawking, the smell of tarweed. They came across his being and were clear but incomprehensible, like the pain. What ceiling, what room, what voices, why. It didn't matter, it was all at a remove from him, none of it concerned him. A man he knew, MacIver, a girl's face he knew but not who she was. They came, they went. It was easy, careless, peaceful.

. . .

There was a black rectangle in front of him. Just black, just there. Light around it, so it was like a hole in the light. It didn't move. At the same time he saw it, a rhythm began to beat in his head like a hammer. It was made of words.

I, fed with judgment

The black rectangle was right in front of him but he couldn't tell how large it was, how close or far. There was a great pressure on him, paralyzing and sickening him, holding him so he couldn't move. He couldn't get away from the black rectangle. It was there in front of him. It was all there was. The words beat at him. He tried to cry out for help. There was nobody to help him.

to receive a sentence

to re CEIVE a SEN tence
WORSE than a BI ram's

Whether he opened his eyes or shut them there was the black space, the bright glare around it, and the words in the terrible rhythm.

The timbers creaked, he saw the glimmer on them overhead. He tried to cling to that because it was before the judgment, before the sentence, but they were gone, there was dirt in his mouth and the words beating, beating him down.

Looking up, he saw the weak glimmer on the rough pine beams. And that was it. That was all.

I, fed with JUDG ment
in a FLESH ly TOMB
AM

• • •

He came back. MacIver was talking to the girl. He didn't understand what they said. He couldn't. He was being thrown around on long, sickening waves. He was in a ship tossing, creaking, sinking out from under him. In a train swaying, swaying as it ran, running off the track, falling down into the canyon. He tried to call out for help. The wheels were beating out the rhythm he dreaded. Then MacIver's face. Then it was all gone again.

• • •

He came back. Somebody was holding him, an arm around his shoulders, a comforting presence, but he heard something whimpering like a hurt dog. It made him ashamed.

"Hey," she said, "you're here. Aren't you?" She was looking at him from close. He saw the grey-green irises of her eyes and the tiny springy hairs of her eyebrows. He understood her.

He tried to say yes or nod. Great pain closed in on him and he shut his eyes. But he had the understanding. It held him, held him here.

. . .

They'd brought him down from the old mine on a stretcher straight into the house and laid him on the bed.

"What," he said to MacIver.

"Tell you about it later."

"What."

MacIver watched him. Judging. Finally he said, "Cave-in." The way he said it made it sound unimportant. Cowper had to think it out.

"Quake?"

MacIver shook his head once. "We have your notes. You wrote, 'Unsafe at 200 yards.' You'd gone on some past that."

"Damn fool," he wanted to say, meaning himself, but it was too difficult because of his chest. Instead after a while he asked again, "What."

MacIver kept watching him. He reached a judgment.

"Stove you in some, William. Compound in the right leg, three ribs, maybe four, I'm not sure. Right wrist. Contusions and abrasions from here to Peru. Not to mention concussion. Satisfied?"

"Lucky."

"Call that luck?"

"Left-handed."

"God damn," MacIver said softly, like a man admiring an ore vein.

. . .

Goldorado was just another mean little town, but one thing she liked about it was the water, mountain springwater clear as air. The house had a standpipe in the yard and water piped to a faucet in the kitchen sink. Mornings, after emptying the chamber pots in the outhouse, she could rinse them clean right there at the standpipe. The plentyness of water made housework easy and bathing luxurious. She could clean up and cool down whenever she felt like it, and do the same for her patient. These hot days there wasn't much cross draft in his room even when she opened the front door, and having to lie in bed with his leg and arm all splinted and bandaged, hardly able to move, he got sweaty and miserable. Doc Mac gave her a bottle of rubbing alcohol to use where it was important not to get the dressings wet, and she took to sponging him off a couple of times a day. Anything cool was pleasant in the July afternoons, and there was nothing disagreeable about the job itself.

Treating Roy's carbuncles had been disgusting, the sores, and the hair that grew all over his shoulders and back like a mangy old buffalo robe, and Roy always either moaning or cussing dirt at her for hurting him. She hadn't seen a lot of men and it was interesting to learn Mr. Cowper's body and compare it to the few others she'd seen. He didn't have a potbelly like Roy. Pete had a lot of wiry gold hair all over him and was milky white where he wasn't tanned. Where it wasn't all bashed and bruised, Mr. Cowper's skin was an even pale brown, like baked bread instead of dough. He was neat, somehow, like an animal. Doing for him had never been hard as soon as she learned what needed doing.

Having to learn it had come unexpectedly. But when had she ever been able to expect anything?

They'd brought him down from the old mine on a stretcher straight into the house and laid him on the bed that had been her and Pete's bed. A whole crowd came in after them, the little house was jam full of people, men women and children all jabbering with excitement about the accident. A couple of dogs got in with the crowd, putting Tiger into a panic fury, so she had to shut him into the kitchen and then into the cubby room, because people kept coming into the kitchen for something that was needed, water or a bowl, or just to stand and chatter about the cave-in. Most of the people had never spoken to Rae since she came there and didn't speak to her now. Then all of a sudden they were gone. Doc Mac had cleared them out.

She knew him from when she'd had to go to him soon after they got to Goldorado, when she was bleeding, losing the baby. He had been kind then, and he always spoke to her in the street.

He stood in the hall when he'd got the door shut on the crowd, and said, "Will you come in here, Miz Tonely?" looking very serious. She followed him into the bedroom. She took a quick look at the man on the bed, not much of him to be seen for bandages. She was glad of that. People had kept saying how he was all torn up and his bones crushed, and she didn't want to see it.

"I need to know if you can help me. He may not make it. I'll do what I can for him, but I need help at it. I need a nurse. I haven't found one yet. He's completely helpless. Have you cared for anybody sick?"

"Some," she said, scared by his hard, fast way of talking.

"I'll try to get a trained nurse up here from Stockton or Sacramento. I'll tell you exactly what to do. I'll get you nurse's wages from his company." What he said came at her so fast she couldn't keep up with it and didn't answer. "There's no place to put him but here," the doctor said with so much trouble in his voice that she said, "I can try."

His face cleared up. He looked at her keenly. She remembered that direct gaze from when she had gone to him with the bleeding. "All right!" he said. "Now let me show you what you'll be doing." He didn't waste any time.

But in the middle of telling her about what she'd be expected to do he stopped as if he'd run out of steam.

"You're a married woman," he said.

She said nothing.

"If you were a girl. But you've seen a man."

After a minute she said, "Yes."

She might have been angry or embarrassed except that he was embarrassed, scowling and fidgeting, and she almost wanted to laugh.

"He will be as helpless as a baby. With the same needs." His voice had gone hard again.

She nodded. "That's all right," she said.

She appreciated Doc Mac for thinking she might be too delicate minded to be able to look at a naked man and tend to his privacies, and the bedpan and all, but she wasn't. And this man was so broken, so beaten, he had been treated so rough that for a while you couldn't see him for his injuries.

She'd never minded having empty time, time by herself. She'd been worrying more than she knew about Pete and money and what next. She could admit to herself now that it was a relief as well as a grief that she'd lost the baby. And Pete.

She didn't have any tears when he went like that, not a word. But she was sad that the good time they'd had ended that way. She'd gotten to feeling scornful of him for always being disappointed and discontented and giving up on things, and she was sorry about that now. He couldn't help the way he was. But anyhow, gone was gone, and she could look ahead again.

It was all right being on her own. Enough money was coming in that she could really save some, enough to take her out of Goldorado. She didn't know where she'd go, her last letter to Aunt Bess had come back stamped No Longer at This Address. But she'd worry about that when the time came.

When there was nothing to do for him and the house was as clean as she cared to bother making it, she would sit in the armchair in his room sometimes with Tiger asleep in her lap and do nothing at all. She'd been worried in this town, and lonely. Now she wasn't. She sat and thought.

She thought again about bodies. She didn't like the word "body." It was the same word for a living person and a corpse. Her own body, or Pete's, which she knew every inch and mole and hair of, or the unconscious damaged body on the bed, were all alive, were what life was. A live body was absolutely different from a dead one, as different as a person from a photograph. The life was the mystery.

A live body was absolutely different from a dead one, as different as a person from a photograph.

And then, holding and handling the hurt helpless man all the time, she was as close to him as she had ever been to Pete, but in a different way. There was no shame in it. There was no love in it. It was need, and pity.

It didn't sound like much, but when you came to the edge between life and death where he was, and she with him, she saw how strong pity was, how deep it went. She'd loved making love with Petey, back when they ran off together, the wanting and fulfilling. It had made everything else unimportant. But the ache of tenderness she felt for her patient did just the opposite, it made things more important. What she and Pete had had was like a bonfire that went up in a blaze. This was like a lamp that let you see what was there.

• • •

It was a while before the doctor would tell him how he'd been found. He couldn't hide his night horrors from Rae Brown, and she told MacIver about them. Maybe he thought they'd be worse if Cowper knew what had happened to him. Cowper was certain that they couldn't be any worse and maybe might be better. So MacIver finally told him.

Ross, the local company manager, had appointed to meet him up at the old Venturado Mine around noon that day to check out what he'd found.

Knowing that, he remembered the climb up to the mine in the morning sunlight, a steep haul through scrub oak and wild lilac that were growing back across the red, rocky scar of the old access road. It was less than a mile from town but felt like wilderness, full of birdsongs and strong scents, young sunlight slanting bright through the pines and tangles of mountain mahogany. The sun was already hot on his shoulders when he saw the mine entrance, a black rectangle in all that brightness.

He had no memory of going in. Nothing. All he had was the creaking in the shaft, the lantern light on the roof beam.

Ross had got there a couple of hours after he did and went into the adit to call him. Going farther in, he saw and smelled the air full of sour dust, and saw Cowper's lantern burning on the floor of the drift just in front of a chest-high tumble of rock and timber. "I thought it was a wall somebody built there," he said. He was looking at it trying to understand what it was when he realized that something blue he saw sticking out from under it was Cowper's shirt sleeve. He was facedown. Ross determined he was breathing. He hauled a couple of the bigger rocks off him but couldn't move the beam across his legs, and hurried back down to town for help.

"He was still wheezing when he located me at Metcalf's treating the old man's piles," MacIver said. "Never seen Ross out of breath and no hat before. Don't expect to again. He's asked about you. But he don't come round to see you."

"I owe him my life, I guess."

"Heaviest debt there is," said the doctor. "Just hope he forgives it."

Cowper brooded for a while. "Who's Abiram?"

"A-byerum? Darn if I know."

"In the Bible, I think."

"Oh well then," MacIver said, "damned if I know, and damned if I don't."

> He was such a gentlemanly drunk it took Cowper a while to realize that he was killing himself.

"Miz Brown?"

"In here," she called from the kitchen.

"You got a Bible?"

She came to the doorway of the room wiping her hands down her apron. "Oh, no, Mr. Cowper, I don't, I'm sorry." She really was sorry, wanting to amend her fault. She was like that, like a child. "Maybe Mr. Robineau would have a spare one? I'll go by the church and ask him when I go out."

"Thank you," Cowper said.

"But don't bring old Robineau back with you," said MacIver. "If this house is going to get filled with righteousness, I'm out of it."

MacIver made him laugh. When he laughed his chest hurt so sharp the tears came into his eyes.

They had known each other two years ago in Ventura, when Cowper was first with the company. They met at a poker game and liked each other. MacIver had a practice there, but he also had a habit. Cowper had been in a low, lonesome place in his life. He was at a bar most nights. He was always glad to meet up with MacIver. The doctor had a keen wit, never lost his temper, was good company. He was such a gentlemanly drunk it took Cowper a while to realize that he was killing himself.

The company took Cowper on full time and sent him to inspect the Oro Grandy Mine, and he lost track of MacIver.

His first afternoon in Goldorado, he was not feeling encouraged about his stay there. Ross, the company's local boss, was a buttoned-up, all-business man. The kid they'd found for him to rent rooms from was unfriendly. The town had popped up on the strength of a couple of shallow-lode mines and was giving out along with them; the four mines he had been sent to inspect were almost certainly played out or barren holes in the ground. A lot of downtown windows were boarded up, bleak even in the blaze of midsummer. A hound dog lay dead asleep in the middle of Main Street. It looked like a few weeks could be a long time there.

The doctor came out of the bank building, saw him, and said, "William Cowper," half questioning, as if not quite certain he had the name or the man right. When Cowper greeted him he looked relieved. He also looked like he'd been through the mangle. Otherwise he was much as he had been, and they picked up easily and pleasantly where they'd left off. Heading off the inevitable invitation to have one at the Bronco or the Nugget, MacIver made it clear that he wasn't drinking. "Where do you get a real dinner here?" Cowper asked him instead. They went off to the hotel and dined early, but in style, with a white tablecloth, oysters, and chicken-fried steak. They drank each other's health in seltzer water.

• • •

She had gone back to sleeping in her bed in the little back room off the kitchen. The walls were thin, and she left the doors open so she could keep an ear out. When he first started having the horrors and screamed out and thrashed trying to get up, she'd been scared of him, afraid she couldn't keep him from hurting himself or hurting her. But he still couldn't get up, and didn't have much strength even in a panic. Once when she was trying to calm him down he flailed out his arm and struck her on the face. It hurt, and she had a bruise next morning. She thought she might have to explain it. Like her mother when Roy hit her, it was just an accident, I was a little tipsy, we both were, he didn't mean any harm. But Mr. Cowper really hadn't meant any harm. It wasn't her he was trying to fight off or get away from. When she could get him to quiet down he was so worn out and confused he didn't know what he'd been doing or who he was talking to. Sometimes he was in tears like a child, crying, "I'm sorry, I'm sorry!" His tears meant he was out of the nightmare, coming back to himself. She liked to watch that relief happening, the mind coming back into his eyes, the quietness into his face. He always thanked her.

She didn't know anything about him of course, but she thought he was a lonely man. He didn't complain about the pain he was in, he joked and toughed that out the way a man expected himself to. But there was a grief in him that showed in his face. It went away when he talked with anybody, but it always came back, it was his look when he was by himself. Desolate.

She knew that word, like so many others, from Aunt Bess. "Oh my sakes, this is a desolate place!" Aunt Bess had cried out once, her first look at one of the dusty little east Colorado towns Roy kept moving them to. She had been so upset Rae hadn't asked her what the word meant then, but later on she had, and Aunt Bess said, "It means alone. Sad. Forsaken." And she'd said some of a poem that started, *Desolate, oh desolate!*

It was a lonesome word. "Forsaken" was even lonesomer. She valued words like that and the people who said them, Aunt Bess, old Mr. Koons, some of the schoolteachers she'd had, the boardinghouse lady in Holt. She had treasured her McGuffey Readers with stories and poems in them. They got left behind in one of the moves to a new town. After that she knew she had to keep what she learned in her head. Even if she didn't say them, knowing words for things she felt and knowing there were people who said them used to help some when she was feeling desolate and forsaken, in those places, in those days.

She hadn't had friends her own age, and envied those who did. She'd used to think the girls just didn't like her, but now she could see that her stepfather and his friends had put them on the outside right away in every town he'd moved them to. Just after they'd come to Grand Junction, Aunt Bessie had had to go back to Kansas to nurse Grandmother Brown, who was dying. She wanted to take Rae with her and Rae wanted to go, but Roy wouldn't have it. Soon after Aunt Bessie left, Roy started bringing his new friend Mr. Van Allen over several nights a week. Rae's mother entertained Mr. Van Allen and the rent got paid.

Girls Rae had begun to know at school stopped speaking to her. It didn't seem to her it was her fault what her mother did. In fact she didn't think it was really her mother's fault. After Daddy died, when Rae was eleven, Mother had done nothing but cry, and before the year was out she married Roy Daid, as if he was the answer to anything. Mother wasn't strong, like Aunt Bessie was. Not everybody was strong. But people wouldn't speak to them now, and the neighbor woman said out loud to somebody in the street, "I'm not used to living next door to a slut."

Rae was so angry at everybody by then she wouldn't let anybody even try to speak to her. There was nobody. Nobody till Pete Tonely showed up with some of Roy's business friends. He was so different. Younger, and really handsome. He didn't hound her and paw her like Roy's friends tried to, but she knew he noticed her a lot. The day after she turned eighteen and found that Sears Roebuck had turned her off from her warehouse job there, Pete had come over. He said something nice to her, and she started crying. She made herself stop crying right away, and they sat out on the back steps talking for a long time. He said, "Rae, I came over to tell you. I'm pulling up stakes. Going to Denver. Tonight." She just sat there, dumb. He took her hand and said, "Listen. I want to take you out of this. If you want to come. I thought about going on to Frisco." She met him down at the train station that night.

> ### Rae's mother entertained Mr. Van Allen and the rent got paid.

The first year had had a lot of excitement in it, and joy. She didn't forget that. But poor Pete was always finding wonderful new friends and new prospects and then they didn't pan out. He got fired, or he quit. As time went on, it seemed like nothing satisfied him anymore. He was never hard on her, but the joy was all gone out of it. A few months after they got anywhere, he was talking about pulling up stakes. When they were in Chico, he'd met some man from a mining town who told him what a great job bartending was, and good money in the tips. And so she'd ended up in Goldorado. Still on the outside.

· · ·

He turned away and strutted off like a turkey gobbler.

Mr. Cowper's boss came one afternoon. She made sure Mr. Cowper had his shirt on and was sitting up, and then left Mr. Ross with him. She went to the kitchen to start dinner. She couldn't help but hear what they said. She didn't much like Mr. Ross, a pink-faced man with cold eyes. He was a gentleman but it wasn't the same kind of gentleman as Doc Mac and Mr. Cowper.

She heard him tell Mr. Cowper that the company was going to keep on paying him while he was laid up. He said, "They think very highly of you down in Sacramento, Cowper," and you could tell that he tried to say it nicely, although it was a strain on him to do so and it came out sounding superior. That warmed her to Mr. Ross.

He chilled her down right away. As she showed him out he said, "No doubt you know, Mrs. Tonely, that your husband has several creditors here who would appreciate knowing when he might return."

Nobody in their senses would have made Pete a real loan. If he'd borrowed money privately that was none of Mr. Ross's business. Unless it was Ross he owed. But Ross wouldn't have lent Pete money any more than the bank would. He had spoken out of pure meanness.

She let her eyes cross his pink face without looking at it, the way he always did to her, and said, "My name's Rae Brown, Mr. Ross. I don't have a husband."

That shocked him maybe more than she meant it to. His pink cheeks went dark red and his jaw shook up and down. He turned away and strutted off like a turkey gobbler.

Well, she certainly was parading her shame. First to Doc Mac, then Ross. Might as well announce, "I was living in sin!" with a megaphone like they had at the rodeo.

She went in and passed Mr. Cowper's door without speaking to him to see if he needed anything. In the kitchen she stood there for a while and felt her face burn red hot. Going around announcing her name, as if being Rae Brown was something to be proud of. It didn't make any difference if she wasn't ashamed. Other people were. They were ashamed for her, of her, that she lived among them. They blushed for her. Their shame was on her, a weight, a load she couldn't get out from under.

· · ·

"All right, let 'er buck."

MacIver handled the book like it might go off if he wasn't careful. He got his finger on the page and line he wanted, grimaced, and began to read in a jerky mumble.

> And Moses sent to call Dathan and Abiram, the sons of Eliab: which said, We will not come up:
>> Is it a small thing that thou hast brought us up out of a land that floweth with milk and honey, to kill us in the wilderness, except thou make thyself altogether a prince over us?
>> Moreover thou hast not brought us into a land that floweth with milk and honey, or given us inheritance of fields and vineyards: wilt thou put out the eyes of these men? we will not come up.

"This making any sense to you?"

"Well, it might if you didn't read it like you were spitting gravel."

"I am not a reading man, William," the doctor said with dignity. "Given time, I have made sense of a medical text. But what's all this stuff? Which, and thou, and putting out eyes?"

"I don't know. If I could look at that book I might could figure it out. But it's not a one-handed book."

"Never heard it mentioned as such," MacIver said. "Hey, Rae?"

"She's hanging out the wash."

MacIver went to call out from the back door. "Rae! You ever done any Bible reading?"

Cowper heard her cheerful voice call back, "I used to read it to my auntie sometimes."

"Will you come make sense of this stuff to the divinity student in here?"

MacIver came back and she followed him. The smell of sunlight on newly washed sheets came in with her and she was laughing. "You two are reading the *Bible*?"

"Not real successfully," Cowper said. "Maybe you could help us out."

She took the thick, heavy, black-bound, red-edged book the minister had lent them. She held it with affectionate respect. "I haven't seen this for a long time. It's just like the one my aunt had."

"Don't lose the place! We had enough trouble finding it! See, there? It's called Numbers 15. Now just start there, and look out for the whiches."

She sat down in the straight chair, studied the page for a minute, and began to read. She read slowly, hesitating over a word now and then—*wroth, tabernacle*—but easily and with understanding. There was a music in it. A couple of times she glanced up to see if they wanted her to go on.

> And Dathan and Abiram came out, and stood in the door of their tents, and their wives, and their sons, and their little children.
>
> And Moses said, Hereby ye shall know that the Lord hath sent me to do all these works; for I have not done them of mine own mind.
>
> If these men die the common death of all men, or if they be visited after the visitation of all men; then the Lord hath not sent me.
>
> But if the Lord make a new thing, and the earth open her mouth, and swallow them up, with all that appertain unto them, and they go down quick into the pit; then ye shall understand that these men have provoked the Lord.
>
> And it came to pass, as he had made an end of speaking all these words, that the ground clave asunder that was under them:
>
> And the earth opened her mouth, and swallowed them up, and their houses, and all the men that appertained unto Korah, and all their goods.
>
> They, and all that appertained to them, went down alive into the pit, and the earth closed upon them: and they perished from among the congregation.
>
> And all Israel that were round about them fled at the cry of them: for they said, Lest the earth swallow us up also.

She looked at Cowper, and stopped.

After a minute MacIver said, "Whatever this Dathan and Abiram did, their wives and sons and little children didn't, did they? That's awful stuff."

Cowper was having some trouble breathing. The doctor had his eye on him as he went on. "You read like an angel, Miss Rae. You come of a religious family?"

"Oh my sakes no. Aunt Bessie and I read her Bible because she liked to be read to when she was sick and there wasn't anything else in the house. Then a neighbor heard she wanted something to read and brought over a whole box full of cowboy adventure stories."

"Made a change from Moses and Korah and them, anyhow." He got up and came over to Cowper. "Got trouble, William?"

Cowper nodded.

"I'll go finish the wash," Rae said, and slipped out, leaving the Bible on the side table. A black rectangle. Cowper shut his eyes and tried to breathe.

Lying there in the long afternoons with nothing but time on his hands he felt what time was.

• • •

He went down into the pit, the earth swallowed him. But he was buried above ground.

• • •

Lying there in the long afternoons with nothing but time on his hands he felt what time was. It was his element, like air. It was a gift. His breath had begun to come easily again, the gift restored. He watched the slow unceasing changes of the light on the walls and ceiling and in the sky out his window. He watched July becoming August. The hours washed over him soft as the mild air.

Angus MacIver came in one morning, told him he'd been lying around like a hog in a wallow long enough, and began teaching him exercises to keep his muscles from wasting and get some strength in the good leg and arm. He did them faithfully, but doing anything at all both exhausted him and made him impatient to be doing more. It made the possibility of getting up off the damn bed, walking, walking back into the world, imaginable. But imagining it now, when it wasn't possible, threatened his gift of ease, made him restless. Doing nothing, he could let peace flow back into him.

And often now the peace lasted through the night. He would wake at what had been his worst hour, just before the turn of night toward day, black dark, the town and the hills dead silent, and watch the stars in his window grow paler and fewer and the chairs and bureau and doorway taking on substance, a long untroubled wakening.

He knew he counted on the doctor visiting most days, sitting down and talking a while, but he hadn't known how much until MacIver went off on one of his rounds, out to people on ranches up in the hills and at the big sawmill down the creek where, as he said, the hands kept practising their sawing on themselves.

Some part of Angus MacIver had a fence around it that was posted "Keep Out."

MacIver didn't keep a horse, renting a mare and a buckboard from Hugh at the livery stable for his rounds, or a riding horse for an emergency when the patient couldn't get into town. Rae said that he was liked and respected in Goldorado, but Cowper had wondered if his practice there was enough to live on. He was open about things like money that some men wouldn't talk about, so Cowper asked him. MacIver told him that two years ago a friend had given him a half interest in a going lumber business over in the redwood country. "Staked me for life," he said. "I'm in the clover. So long as people keep building houses."

"Man doesn't get many friends like that," Cowper said, thinking of Mr. Bendischer.

MacIver nodded, but his face closed down. Some part of Angus MacIver had a fence around it that was posted Keep Out. No barbed wire, but the sign was clear from a distance. It just wasn't clear to Cowper what was inside it.

Talking about himself to get away from whatever had shut MacIver down, he had said, "I got staked like that. When I was a kid." He stopped. He didn't want to tell the story.

But MacIver wanted to hear it. "Ran away from home?"

"My parents died. In a train wreck." He stopped again, but couldn't leave it there. He had to make his recitation. "On a switchback. My father worked for the Tomboy Mine up there. Near Ouray. The track had buckled since the last inspection. On a downgrade. Engine went off the rails down into the canyon and took the first car with it. They were in it. Me and my sister had gone back to the last car. The observation platform."

"How old were you?"

"Cleo was fourteen. I was eleven."

MacIver waited.

"Well, our next of kin was my mother's uncle. He took me and my sister with him to Pueblo. Then he fixed it up somehow with the bank and skipped out with everything Father left us." He heard his voice dull and level, like a rote recitation in school. "There was an old lawyer there in Pueblo, he'd have liked to get our uncle to justice. He tried. Couldn't do it. But he took an interest in my sister and me. Cleo wanted to work and keep me in school, and he helped her do that. He saved us. Robert Bendischer. I honor his name. He put me through the mining school in Golden. Mrs. Bendischer never liked us."

"How about your sister?"

"Cleo died of diphtheria. Two years after our parents."

After a while MacIver said, "God moves in a mysterious way." He had asked his questions gently, but spoke now with savage bleakness.

When he left that day he put his arm around Cowper's shoulders. In his helplessness the doctor had handled him all the time, deft and gentle. This was different, awkward, a sudden half embrace that hurt. MacIver left without a word, scowling.

He had been away five days now. It seemed like nothing happened and nothing changed. He did his exercises, but they didn't get easier, and except for the scabs healing over he didn't feel he was getting any better. His leg and wrist were still in heavy bandages, immobile, hot in the long hot afternoons and evenings. His side still hurt and his breath came short when he moved. Even the bruises didn't seem to fade much. He still needed Rae to help him do anything at all.

She was good at thinking of what he might need and asking him about it or just doing it. He knew that and appreciated it. But he was so sick of still having to ask, can you do this, will you do that, that he didn't always treat her the way he ought to. She was patient with his crankiness up to a point. Then she went silent, and when she'd done what was needed she'd leave him silently, going to another room or outside. But always in hearing.

When she had to leave the house, she told him, and made sure there was somebody within earshot, usually the ten-year-old from the only other house on South Fifth Street, a shy boy who wouldn't meet your eyes. Tim always brought with him a game board that had a star design with indentations for marbles. He sat for hours moving the marbles into patterns. It should by rights have driven Cowper mad to watch the poor kid, but in fact he found that silent absorption soothing. And he wanted soothing. He was losing the sweet, idle flow of uncounted time. Often now he felt irritable, babyish, stupidly emotional, finding himself often in a fit of anger, or a panic, or halfway to tears. He lay there listening to the endless chorus of grasshoppers out on the dry, hot, gold hillsides, sweating, comfortless, desperately pushing despair away. Then Rae would come in and smile. She didn't hold grudges any more than the cat. He was glad to see her, glad she was there. He didn't know how to say so, but she seemed to be glad to see him and be there, so it wasn't necessary.

There was still nothing much to do but think. He found he had a good supply of things to think about. What went on outside the house in this town he scarcely knew, and it didn't concern him, so he thought mostly about the past and about what was there right now, like Rae.

Whoever the handsome sullen kid was who'd been there with her, he'd evidently walked out, but she didn't seem like her heart was broken. She wasn't much more than twenty and had the stunning health and grace and glow of her age, but she didn't have the self-consciousness girls had, that always tied him up in knots. She wasn't hard, but in a way she was sophisticated. Maybe more than he was. He felt that sometimes, although he must be ten years older than she was. Or it was that she was a woman. Like Cleo, she knew what had to be done and went on and did it. A lot of what she had to do for him was embarrassing to him, shameful. It would have been unbearable if she'd felt the same way about it. She didn't. She took necessity for granted. She was grown up.

Cleo. A steady kindness. A buoyancy. A spring rising.

Thinking of her brought them all together into his mind, his sister and father and mother. Their good nature, their good cheer. It was like a fire-lit room. His memory of it was a window that showed it to him warm and bright. But there was no door, no way back in. They were alive there. He was the ghost, whimpering outside in the dark.

He hadn't left that room by choice, but men did. Probably he would have. A man went off alone to prove he wasn't soft. Didn't let himself depend on anybody. Didn't let down with anybody, didn't trust them, because that gave them the advantage over him. Cowper had lived in a man's world since before he was one himself. It was all the world that was left to him. The job cut out for him was a man's job: to fight the battle of life, to compete, succeed, win. Mr. Bendischer had talked about that with him, and had given him the weapons and the armor he needed for the battlefield. And so far he'd done all right.

But what a barren life it was. Always farther from the firelit room.

He liked his work. He was satisfied by knowing what he was doing and doing it well. But to most of the people who ran things, the men who kept the battle of life going, that wasn't enough, wasn't what it was all about.

Men dug tunnels after gold, he thought, but they didn't build them right. If they'd take pity on each other and themselves, they'd build right. At least shore up their ratholes with timber you could count on.

His thoughts went winding around that way, following each other's tails, and the afternoon would pass while he let them lead his mind back to paths it used to walk long ago and places it hadn't been before. He must have been needing some time to think, to take stock, because coming out of one of those long reveries he felt peaceful again, and it didn't seem so bad to be stuck helpless and useless in a bed in a hot little room in a half-dead little town in Amador County, California.

Holding his mind away from the beat of the terrible words, he sat up and watched daylight slowly transform the sky.

Then in the night he woke facedown with dirt in his mouth and eyes, blind, paralyzed, trying to get his breath with no breath, and the beat pounding in his ears. Buried above ground.

He struggled awake, struggled to calm himself. Holding his mind away from the beat of the terrible words, he sat up and watched daylight slowly transform the sky.

He knew he'd be afraid to go to sleep that night. He thought about it all morning. When he slept there was no way to keep it from happening. He'd learned something about keeping off the horrors, but he had to be awake to do it.

Reciting poetry he'd learned by heart in school and singing songs in his head, it didn't matter what, "Red River Valley" or "Praise God, from Whom," could keep him from slipping into the awful rhythm. If he could get "The boy stood on the burning deck" going, even that could keep

Abiram away. He wished they'd made him memorize more in school. He lay hunting for bits of poetry and tunes that had been stuck deep in his mind like little gold veins in granite since before he could remember. "The cow's in the meadow, the sheep's in the corn . . ."

He'd ask Angus to find him something to read. He'd manage holding a book and turning the pages somehow. What the hell, he was an engineer, couldn't he figure out something that would hold a book where he needed it?

"Are there any books in the house, Rae?"

"Just yours," she said. "You want some more to drink?"

She refilled his glass from the pitcher on the bureau and set it on the crate they'd rigged up as a table, which he could reach with his left hand. The bed was close to the wall so that now he could sit up he could see more than sky out the window. His view was an old plum tree in the side yard and a triangle of Sierra foothill forested with white oak, scrub oak, madrone, and a couple of Jeffrey pines. To get to the crate-table Rae had to go between the bedside and the wall. The windowsill stuck out so she had to squeeze past it a little, turning sideways, away from him. Watching her hips and buttocks negotiate that passage in and then back out was an unfailing pleasure.

> She turned burning red, fire red, face, ears, throat, whatever could be seen of her.

"I guess you gave that Bible back."

"Did you want to hear some more?"

"I liked hearing you read it."

"I like reading. I read a lot to my aunt when she was sick. I can borrow it back from Mr. Robineau."

"Maybe something that isn't the Bible," he said.

"There's some books in your other room."

He thought about it. "Materials stress resistance calculation tables are on the dry side."

She said, not turned toward him as she said it, "There's some other books in your trunk."

His trunk, what he'd put in it packing it in San Francisco. Another world. "What are they?" he asked more of himself than her.

"A poetry book and a book by Charles Dickens."

"Ace in the hole!" He was delighted. "Fetch 'em in here, Rae!" Of course he'd brought the Dickens—he'd bought it in the city to bring here, thinking there might be some long evenings. And he'd traveled with Cowper's *Poems* so long he'd forgotten about it.

Rae turned around. He saw with surprise that she had gone red, which with her was no modest-maidenly-pink business. She turned burning red, fire red, face, ears, throat, whatever could be seen of her. Then, more slowly, she turned white and stayed that way for some time. He'd seen her go through this once before, but not so extremely as now. It was distressing, and he felt sorry for her and sorry about causing the distress. But he had no idea what he'd said to cause it. Had he told her to fetch the books like an order?

"Mr. Cowper, I had to unlock your trunk and look in it. A while ago. I had to."

"That's all right with me, Rae." His first thought was that there was nothing of any value in the trunk, then he remembered he'd stuck some bills and coins in under the other stuff. Trying to ease her disproportionate embarrassment, he said, "If you ever get short of cash money, there's some in the bottom, did you find that?"

She burst into tears. The tears ran down her pale face. The sobbing shook her hard. She cried like a child, openly. It had come on her so suddenly she couldn't hide it and didn't try. She just stood there weeping. He tried to reach out to her but of course couldn't get anywhere near her. All he could say was her name, don't cry, it's all right.

She got the sobbing under control and with one of his handkerchiefs from the top bureau drawer wiped her eyes and nose. Doing that allowed her to turn away from him for a while. When she turned back she was still pale, and she'd missed some of the snot on her left cheek. He had never felt pity so sharp, so urgent, pity like a knife stab. It made him reach out to her again, sitting up and turning as much in the bed as he was able to. She saw his gesture, but did not put out her hand to his, though she came a little closer to the bed and tried to smile.

"I was afraid Pete might have taken your money. It's all right, it's there. He didn't. I hid the key. I wasn't sure if Pete might come back." She frowned and her mouth drew back in a grimace repressing another rush of tears.

"Well you did just right," he said, talking to her as if she were a child, letting his useless right arm drop back to his side, feeling his own tears ache in his throat and behind his eyes. "You did just right, Rae. Thanks."

Something relaxed between them then. An inner movement, very deep down, definitive, almost imperceptible.

She poured a little water from the white tin pitcher into the washbasin on the bureau and splashed her face and used his handkerchief with better success. She took the basin out to the front door to toss the water onto the scraggly rosebush by the steps. She came back into the room and said resolutely, "See, when he left, he took my money. So I was afraid maybe he'd—I'm sorry, Mr. Cowper."

Nothing came to him to say to her but, "That's all right." Then, "Look, Rae. We could drop the Mr, maybe. My name's William."

She stood looking at him. Head cocked, but serious. Judging. "I guess I can do that," she said. She did not smile. "Thank you."

. . .

When Doc Mac came in, she was sitting close to the lamp so she could go on reading *Little Dorrit* aloud. William was sitting up in bed. The old cat was asleep on the bed by his legs. "Well this is a pleasant domestic scene," Doc said with a grin, looking in from the dark of the hallway at them in the glow of yellowish light.

"Hey Angus," William said, and she could hear how glad he was to see him. "It's been a while."

"Bunch of fools out there in the sticks. Everything wrong with 'em from scurvy to bunions to a ten-month pregnancy. They need looking after."

"Did you get any dinner, Doc? We've got some pork and beans left I could quick heat up, and corn bread—"

"Thanks, Rae, they fed me at the Mannhofers'. Klara's a good cook, I generally try to get there around a mealtime. How's your sixth costa vera doing, William?"

"It'll do. You missed a shindy, Saturday night."

"Heard something about it. The Edersons again, right? I keep hoping someday some of that lot will manage to murder at least a few of each other."

"Carl Ederson went to shoot his brother Peer but he hit his cousin's horse. Or he was trying to shoot the horse and hit Peer. Which is it, Rae?"

He made her laugh. "Nobody really knows what happened," she said. "Just that Erland's horse got shot, and then Carl left town. And old Mr. Ederson says he's going to shoot Carl soon as he sees him. And old Mrs. Ederson threw his gun into the creek." They were all laughing. Coming past her to sit down in the straight chair, Doc touched her shoulder, a little light brush of the hand, the way he did sometimes. It was close in the small room. She and Doc were near the lamp, batting off or slapping at tiny mosquitoes. William was sitting up against the pillows, and his strong profile partly in the yellow light and part in deep shadow looked like an old photograph or a stone carving.

"I came in on a reading," Doc said. "More of the Scriptures? You trying to figure out what Abiram actually did to bring God down on him and his wife and the babies?"

"No," William said. "Don't reckon I ever will. We're reading the Gospel by Dickens."

"*Pickwick Papers*? I saw a play made out of that in KC once."

"This is *Little Dorrit*. More on the serious side."

"Well give me a shot of it. I am tired, to tell you the truth. Sitting here getting read to by a beautiful woman sounds like just what the doctor ordered." She tried to beg off, but he meant it. "Go on from where you were." Rae picked up the book and found her place.

> "See, when he left, he took my money. So I was afraid maybe he'd—I'm sorry, Mr. Cowper."

• • •

"He's asleep."

"I know. Just go on reading."

"He's going to fall off the chair."

Doc started, half stood up, shook his head, sat down, and woke up. "Well, God damn, I went to sleep!" he said, and then, "Rae, I'm sorry. I am truly sorry."

She thought he was apologizing for going to sleep. She had got so used to Roy and the men he knew and then Pete and the men he knew cursing all the time, language a lot worse than "damn," which she hadn't even noticed. When she understood, she was embarrassed and touched, and said at random, "You didn't know what you were saying. I don't mind. You must be worn out. I was getting tired reading, anyhow."

"Foul-mouthed old cuss," William said. "Can't have you around the ladies. Go home and go to bed. We're all pie-eyed. It must be past midnight."

"It is," Doc said, looking at his silver watch. "Thank you for the fine entertainment." He yawned enormously. "Good night!"

He lurched out, waving the back of his hand at them vaguely.

"Never thought it had got so late," William said.

"I love that man," Rae said. "He's just good."

She felt dreamy, half there, half in the story she had been reading to them. She got Mr. Cowper—she still called him that in her head when "Mr. Cowper" made things easier than "William" did—seen to for the night, blew out the lamp, and bade him good night.

It seemed pitch dark for a moment, but the starlight and an old moon just clearing the mountains made a grey light in the house, enough for him to find his chamber pot if he had to, and for her to get to bed, still in the half dream of the story.

He'd been such a short time in Goldorado before the tunnel fell in on him that he didn't have much picture of the town.

It tickled her that Doc had called her a beautiful woman. She knew that from him it meant nothing except his kindness. But for some reason she was glad he'd said it front of William.

As she undressed the story came back around her. It had been hard going at first when they were all in Marseille, which she had to remember to pronounce Marsay, and the prison there, and the quarantine. She could see the places, but what was going on didn't begin to make much sense until the third chapter, called "Home," when Arthur Clennam was with his mother in the old house. And then when the story got to Mr. Dorrit and Amy and her sister in the Marshalsea Prison. She had gone right on tonight to the chapter called "The Lock" because she didn't want to stop, even though she knew it was late. Arthur Clennam followed Amy to the prison and met Amy's father, and then she had to stop reading because Doc was tilting over in his chair like a tree about to fall. That room and her bedroom were all mixed up in her head with Mr. Dorrit, and his brother Frederick, and Amy bringing her dinner for her father to eat. Jail cells and old dark places with heavy doors locked on the fragile human souls inside them. And the sweet night air pouring down the mountains through the house. She began going to sleep before she'd gotten all the way into bed.

• • •

It was a Sunday morning. He knew because things had been very loud at the Nugget last night and didn't quiet down till late, after the cricket trilling died away. Anyhow it felt like Sunday. And presently they began hymn-singing away down Main Street in Mr. Robineau's church. He'd been such a short time in Goldorado before the tunnel fell in on him that he didn't have much picture of the town. He remembered or imagined a little clapboard chapel with a kind of halfhearted try at a steeple. The congregation sounded pretty thin on the ground from the way they wailed out a hymn he didn't know, or maybe he couldn't tell what it was because half of them were out of tune and all of them singing it like a dirge. Why did people drag out hymns like that? A good hymn deserved a good tempo. They went caterwauling on and on, it always sounded like the last verse at last, but it never was. Sitting up straight, breathing easy, and feeling good in the bright morning light already warming the air, he sang to show how it should be done—not loud, but moving right along with the beat. He sang his own hymn.

> God moves in a mysterious way.
> His wonders to perform;
> He plants His footsteps in the sea
> And rides upon the storm.

Rae was in the doorway, bright-eyed, half laughing. Cowper waved his left hand like a choirmaster and sang on.

> Deep in unfathomable mines
> Of never failing skill,
> He treasures up His bright designs
> And works His sov'reign will.

He stopped and looked at her. "Cowper's Hymn," he said.
"Go on!"
"That's the part I like. It's in the book, if you want to read it." He reached for the smaller book that she had fetched from his trunk along with *Little Dorrit*. She had put them both on his crate-table, and the smaller one had stayed there. He held it out to her. She was shy about taking it from him, so he opened it to the title page. Before that was the flyleaf, with the inscription on it in spidery legal writing, *To my dear young friend and namesake of the Poet, William Cowper, on the occasion of his matriculation. May you find Honor and Contentment in your chosen profession. September 1889. R.E. Bendischer.* He knew it without

reading it. He showed Rae the title page, and then turned to the hymn. It took a while, one-handed, but he knew the page. He knew all the pages.

"He called it 'Light Shining out of Darkness,' but mostly it gets called 'Cowper's Hymn.'"

She took the book from him at last.

"I never heard you sing," she said.

"I didn't feel much like it lately."

"I guess not." She was still shy, not looking at the book, or at him. He never could figure out her shynesses, her embarrassments. They were mysteries. The more he knew Rae, the more her mysteries. Endless. Unfathomable.

"I like that word," she said. She was blushing some, but went ahead. She was looking down at the open book now. "It's a grand word. *Unfathomable.*"

After a while Cowper said, "It is." 🛡

CHURCH OF

I.

Church of why have I never before, before eating, said aloud the
gratitudes I so keenly feel.

Church of no time like the present.

In hawk-light, kill-light, church delivering hunger unto the body, and
also ground for searching.

Church founded on horseshit dried gold, frost in the folds of leaves, ridges
and hollows if you take a mouse-view—if you take that view, there are
crenelations enough for all to tuck in and sleep safe, both eyes closed.

Church of muscle and talon unhinged from thought.

Of everything connected by *and* and *and*. (Elizabeth Bishop)

2.

Church of no grass growing under *her* feet. (my mother)

Of, in translation from the German, the Schwäbisch, and heard at least
weekly, *Donner wetter nach a mal*, meaning *here we go again with the storm*
(my great-aunt), meaning me.

Well, no, from where I sit, prayer's more sidereal: *Bright Star, would I were
as steadfast as thou art* (Keats)—meaning make of me a navigable point,
fasten me, steady me.

Church of St. Somebody-in-the-Fields, and what all's hidden for the
go-seekers, in the corners-of, fatted on gleanings—

—those protections I found: blue glass eye for staring down evil, blue
feather, no sign of the one who gave it. Those *portions*. And that they
showed up together. I'm listening.

Church of ear-pressed-to-the-wall to better follow the terrible
arguments (that one's a child-filled church).

Wherein shadows hold their breath. (Emily Dickinson)

Church of the tossed family photos. May they rest. Light in the morning,
   slant through high windows, squinting back says: *All of them tossed,*
   every one of them? Yes. Every one. Gone.

Church of I am wide awake now.

St. Girl-in-the-Fields, Girl-in-a-Tree.

3.

St. Red Hickory, sprung from the side of the Indian mound in the
   cemetery in Marietta, OH. I climbed the forty stone steps thinking
   why ok to climb up the sacred. And sit. On the, I am not kidding,
   bench fastened there. Names cut in the hickory, now visible. The hurt
   of that. Small-seeming in the scope of wrongnesses.

Let me resize it then:

Church of you *fuckers*, look up *ploughshares*, look up *swords, spears, pruning*
   hooks. Read the *whole passage*. And also *what you do unto-the-least-of, to*
   water, air, memory, that we are, all of us, rhizomatic. Your fucking greatness.

Church of you got *some* mouth on you, girl.

Church of don't "girl" me and that ain't the half of it—and while I'm in
here, goodbye home church of standard English, immigrant led, fear
fed, must not show it I learned.

Church empurpled by ruckuses, unrest, the rough talk of jays I learned
once, and is coming back now.

4.

—and other Emphatic Pronunciations, say it "Thee" not "the"—as I still
address by hand my envelopes, "To THE one and only (your name
here)"—you, who are famous to me out of love.

Church of the hot attic choir loft, adepts nesting in insulation, all the
old letters, raveling and un. Time licking the envelopes clean of their
glue, brittling up the trifolds inside, the joy-filled and slow-acting,
poison ones, both.

Of the goldfinch, who resembles the body it eats from: the sunflower, its
favorite, wings down. Sunflower, who resembles the source *it* feeds
on, and so it goes with hunger's cosmology—it's not a food *chain* but a
set of right pairings, so all the meant-to-be's end up together.

Much has been spoken in black hoof and owl bone—then came a tangle
   of snakes (*burl* the name the tangle was given) that I, without fear,
   watched climb the tree, bracelet of snakes, boiling up, filling the
   branches, knowing it meant but not *what* . . .

Church whose circumference is everywhere and nowhere at once.
   (Thomas Traherne) ??

Fearsome, how much I like it in here, with One whom I've only just met.

Church of what catches and holds me now, that cap of spiky, black hair.
   Hers. It shines so, is run through with silver, an ore I sift, I put my
   hands in for the current of her.

Wild iris, black-eyed Susans, hellebore down in the yard, and other green
   names I have not yet learned, two crows up there in the white pine,
   girl crows they tell me, but I knew that already.

5.

Those fine red berries of nipples the Renaissance sisters in paintings
   held between fingers, that tautness, tenderness kindled up—in the
   body, which is not an allegory . . .

. . . but itself a church of arching and gnashing, and otherwise, joy in
a good strong piss in the barn, not shy in a stall, right there in the
open. Church of the unabashed horse.

Church of deer legs, feathers, stones (you in the stone, your glacial
advances) come unto my sack, how it happens and keeps on
happening, and no I don't understand, it's unfolding (ear to my
bundle, bundle to chest) as I go, I have to keep going, all I can do
some days just to gather things up, press them close, and quit asking.

Holy, that blood in the cup of my hand, stain of it, iron-salt-yeast of it,
wet with black seeds I dreamed once, with instructions of where
on the body to put it. That I haven't yet, can't yet, and why, is still
coming clear, I have to believe—

—here in the Church of sit your ass down, stay with it, practice,
rage it out, cry it out, that's enough now,

Church of you-listen-to-me-good. (my grandmother again)
Of God never said one word to me. (Maggie's mother)

Of the glorious impedimenta: those ferns of frost grown up overnight on
all the windows, such that their starriness seals me in,

such that I must turn immediately out again.

To crow shine against nightfall blue—the word for that, that won't
come—so I sit inside it and wait. Make that my churchtime.

This morning, walking into a spiderweb was like being anointed with
spit.

Such is the body and the ways of its knowing. That it knows. What it
knows. Can't unknow anymore in the holy wake of, *that* church—

of fireweed, come in after the burning. To purple things up. Counter
what flared. Soften the char.

My own name means purple.

Maybe I'll seed in, maybe I'll leaf out best in the aftermath.

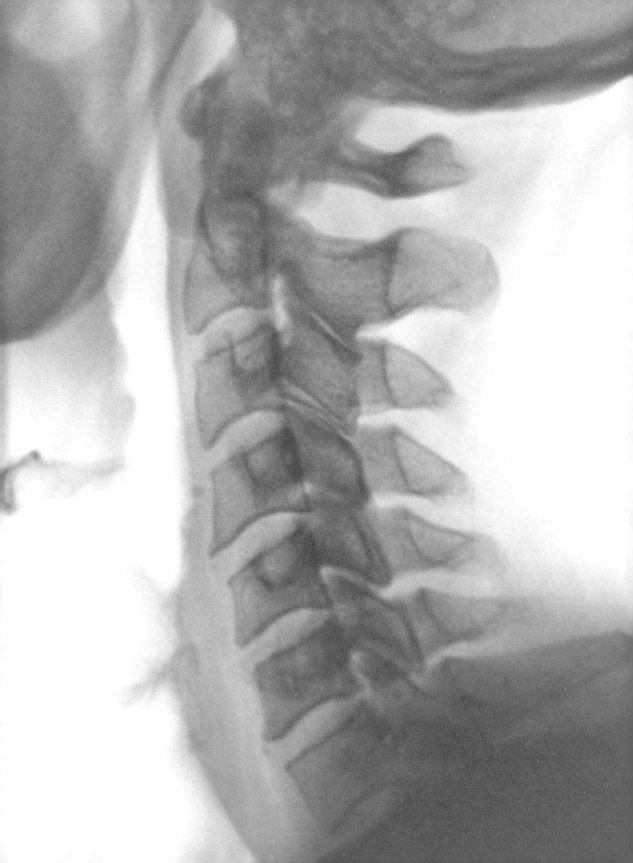

CAN YOU TOLERATE THIS?

Ashleigh Young

This is Spinal Rearrangement

When you go to your chiropractor, he first asks you to take off your necklace. Then he stands behind you and puts his hands around your neck. He squeezes the vertebra at the base of your skull. The vertebra feels tender, as if bruised. "Can you tolerate this?" he asks. You try to nod. You hadn't known that vertebrae could reach so far up, right to the back of the brain.

"Oh yes. The vertebrae go all the way up to the head, like a ladder. Humans are really just highly evolved ladders."

You like the idea that the human body is first and foremost a structure, like flat-pack furniture or a foldaway bed. The ribs, too, go up a long way, into the soft fleshy parts of the back near the armpits.

You lie down on the stretcher, which is a low vinyl-covered table with a head-rest that has two fabric-covered sausages on each side, into the center of which you put your face. From there, in a muffled voice, you talk to your chiropractor: about the foul spring weather, how you were knocked off your bike last week, maybe how you're thinking of quitting your job.

You've known the chiropractor for two years. He's a nice man. He's someone who, when you say something banal—which is often—reacts as if you've said something extraordinary or very funny. But you're not really paying attention to this conversation. It's the other conversation you're interested in: the one between his hands and your back.

Your back feels as if it's listening. You know his hands are close when you feel a tingle in the skin on your back, as if the nerves in your spine are reaching up to the surface.

Your chiropractor begins to knead your spine. You can hear him counting under his breath—T3, T4, T5. Those are some of your thoracic vertebrae, named according to their positions within the spine.

It sounds like torture when you try to describe it to other people. You come here to have your spine shoved or your head wrenched sideways. Better to talk about the lightness and tallness you feel when you leave. Some people are so afraid of chiropractic that they become afraid of *you* if you mention your chiropractor. The difficulty is that a person's life is held, essentially, in the spine. If you mess badly with it, you will die or be paralyzed. Your jaw will seize and your eyes will stare frozenly. For some, chiropractic will never escape those connotations of torture. Mostly it's because we think bones should be silent. When we hear them moving, we think of pain, of permanence.

"Those aren't your bones making that noise," says your chiropractor when you ask. "It's actually gas." It's the sound of tiny bubbles of oxygen, nitrogen, and CO_2—by-products that are formed in the production of the synovial fluid in the joints of the spine. The gas releases from the joint with a *pop*. Nothing ever happens to the bones themselves, the chiropractor says. The bones stay quiet, the introverts of the body.

If you ever ask him a question, it's as if the chiropractor becomes worried that you've grown skeptical and he has to persuade you all over again. So now he explains that the spine is like a scaffold, or a bridge between your nerves and your body, holding all of you upright so that the work of art that is the body can commence motion. He laments the way people say, "I've put my back out," as if a back were something you could hold at arm's length and leave on the curbside. "The problem with people is that they think of themselves as bits and pieces. Go to the gym, work on your pectorals. Work on your quads. A body part here, a body part there. Then we wonder why we feel so disconnected from ourselves. As if your head lives on a different continent from your feet, or your eyes live on a different planet from your heart. Well, for some people perhaps that is figuratively true. But most of us live in the one body, wouldn't you agree? All of those parts are endlessly, infinitesimally connected." He says that if your scaffolding is askew, then the rest of your body and your mind won't work. Things start sliding, shaking, falling. You wake up one morning and you can't move your neck. That's where the manipulations—or, more technically, subluxations—come in. All day long, he is not only fixing but reconnecting.

"I'm not saying there aren't some essential differences between the human body and, say, an airplane. But there aren't very many." He pauses. He's found something, some vertebrae that aren't where they should be. "Deep breath in—and deep breath out—" and he pushes your spine so hard it crackles electrically.

He has you roll to the left. He rearranges your arms so that you're in a relaxed fetal position. Then he presses one of his knees against your thigh—he has large square knees that dwarf your smallish round ones—and pushes. There's a faint cracking sound, like roots pulling up. You imagine fissures appearing in your body as if during a quake.

"Can you tolerate this?"

You keep your eyes half closed but you can see him looming above you like a pylon. "Yup. I'm fine." You roll to the right and he cracks open the other side.

Sometimes, when you're lying here having your vertebrae prodded, he will ask you a question. The question will be big and difficult. It will be something like, "What do you think is the difference between a thought and an emotion?"

You will struggle to answer. But you try to sound as if you think about this kind of thing all the time, as if you're on a slightly different time-space continuum from everybody else. "Well, a thought is only ever in your head. An emotion can be, I don't know, in other places in your body. It can be everywhere. It's kind of shapeless and fluid. It can feel almost physical, like a pain." Your voice sounds all wrong against the stretcher.

He never agrees or disagrees with what you say; instead he pauses for a moment—you can feel him thinking, through his hands—and then says something like, "Could you say, perhaps, that an emotion is a physical thought?"

"I'm not saying there aren't some essential differences between the human body and, say, an airplane. But there aren't very many."

Immediately you wish you had thought of this. "Exactly! An emotion can make you feel sick or sweaty or excited, and those are all like physical expressions of different thoughts."

Talking like this makes you wriggle around, and your chiropractor gently straightens you out or puts your arms back down at your sides.

In the past, like most people, you thought that seeing a chiropractor was an absurd risk. It wasn't until a friend at work, telling you about his own pain, persuaded you that there was something good in this method—something that really worked, maybe even something transformative—that, being desperate with shoulder pain, you decided to reconsider.

At first, it felt like a mistake, this blind trusting of a person, much bigger and stronger than you, with your life. But when you're stretched out on this vinyl table, when your chiropractor puts his hands on your back and tells you what he knows about your bones, then the idea of risk becomes only that: an idea. Something rootless. There's something else, too. This feeling that happens when you are touched. It is a kind of trust in itself. Trust is something that moves about between you, that rises to meet him.

"That back is good to go. Sit up now," he says. You do, fuzzy-haired, squinting; your eyes have adjusted so quickly to the face-down darkness that they feel splintered by light from a window. The sun is angling in. The egg-colored elasticated spine is hanging in the corner. "Let's take a look at that neck of yours."

He looks down at you and takes your head in both hands. He presses your throat just under your jawline, the bones at the base of your skull, and the tender spots under your ears. He gazes over the top of your head. You can't help thinking at this point that, maybe, he will lean down and kiss you. That he will frame your face with his hands and engulf your mouth, warmly, and the office space and the spine hanging in the corner and the anatomical posters on the walls will disappear. There is too little difference between the beginning of a kiss and the beginning of a neck adjustment. You stare at his face, waiting, breathing through your mouth.

After a final pause, he yanks your head to the left—*snap*—then to the right. The sound is a sheet of bubble wrap popping. Your chiropractor steps back and nods, finally looking you in the eye. Now that he's out of your personal space, he is safe.

"You're good at those," he remarks with a wry smile. "Most people scream a little bit."

You try out your new neck: it feels freer, oilier, as if all the synovial fluid has been released to flood over the joints in there.

There is too little difference between the beginning of a kiss and the beginning of a neck adjustment.

And your head sits more lightly, an egg balanced in a spoon.

But wouldn't it be easier to simply feel nothing? It wouldn't be a problem if you could think of your body as an airplane, as your chiropractor does, or simply a lattice of sinew and bone, muscle, soft tissue, nerve fibers. A body with an ordinary skeleton inside it; it could be anyone's, it could be one of those pink-and-white posters on the wall, bristling with pointers and labels.

To mask your lapse, and perhaps to redeem yourself to your chiropractor in case he has sensed what you were thinking during the neck adjustment, you quickly ask another question even though this will hold him up. "Do you ever get annoyed about skeptics? I mean, do you have people who come in and say they think it's all phony but their friend told them to come, that kind of thing?"

"Oh," he says—and you can hear the pragmatism in his voice; he's used to being the reasonable, rational one among the disbelieving—"there's certainly a lot of folklore around. People think they've slipped a disc. They think they've got a nerve floating around in their spine, you know, just drifting around in there. Sometimes when I treat people's backs, they think I've broken them in half! Or they think I'll give them a stroke or a heart attack. But look, I don't waste my energy getting frustrated anymore. You have to look above all that stuff. You have to work above it."

You take your necklace from his desk and put it back on. You always feel a little awkward doing this; this small, intimate putting-on in your chiropractor's office. Briefly you are a woman in a movie.

He is shuffling the pages of his appointment book. "How are you for next Thursday at noon?" Between his eyes is a hearty furrow. How old is he? You're no good at guessing age. The whites of his eyes are properly white, not like the whites of most eyes, which are singed with vessels or nicotine-yellow; in most eyes you can see what people have been looking at: traffic, computer screens, TVs. You find yourself staring at his skin. You can imagine him in one of those multiblade razor ads, the kind where a fighter plane is tearing through the sky. Its body explodes to reveal your chiropractor tensed and helmeted at the controls; the air resistance rips his suit from his body to reveal his bare torso, then he is neatly deposited in an incandescent bathroom as a razor darts through the air and slots into his hand. His face, now magically slathered with shaving foam, appears above the razor.

"Thursday's good for me."

After paying up—twenty-five dollars for fifteen minutes, which you can't really afford—you smile good-bye and he puts his hand lightly on your shoulder, as if placing a full stop there. He is a genuinely nice man. He is interested in people: their bones, their physical thoughts. And you feel the thing you so often feel when you meet someone like this—that you have done nothing to deserve this niceness.

When you're walking down the stairs, you feel a suspicious glow in your belly. It's then you realize: you've got to stop this. Your chiropractor is a mechanic and you are a vehicle in occasional need of repair. When being helped, that is all we need to be. A hairdresser touches hundreds of heads. A doctor listens to hundreds of hearts. None of that means anything beyond what it is.

A month or so down the line, you're greeted at the office by a young woman with a shiny brown ponytail. Your usual chiropractor is away today. The woman has strong hands and enviable self-confidence. She adjusts your lower back, hips, neck, and the sticky-outy rib that is causing your sore shoulder. You leave feeling slightly delirious.

At your next appointment, she tells you that your usual chiropractor is in hospital. He has a tumor. "I just wanted to let you know," she says. "It's early days yet. He's doing fine. We'll just see what happens."

You think of your chiropractor in hospital, waiting for tests, waiting to see what happens. Who does he trust with his life? You wonder what it would be like to visit him. You could take flowers, a book, a card. But, of course, you don't visit. He will already have so many visitors. He will be tired. He will need to sleep between visits.

At each appointment over the next months, the new chiropractor tells you he's doing okay. Then she stops mentioning him, and simultaneously you just stop wondering. It's as if some part of you has decided that he will no longer appear in your life and is shutting down the wondering mechanism. Your new chiropractor has warm, friendly eyes and a ready smile. She knows the parts of your neck that store tension in gnarls (she has something called an Activator gun—it looks like a syringe from hell—that she shoots into each side of your neck); she knows all about the wayward rib; she knows that there are two muscles on either side of your lower spine that are always sore. At first you'd thought they were your kidneys. Sometimes it seems that you don't know your body at all. The names and locations of things. You need someone else to tell you what your body is doing.

At the vegetable market the air is cool from a night of rain. Broken stalks and leaves are scattered on the asphalt among the stalls. People gather and bend and fill seamy plastic bags. You're looking for tomatoes when you see your chiropractor, your old one, bending toward a crate full of apples, sorting through them. You hold back for a second—this could be weird and awkward—then say hello. He looks at you for a few seconds, searching, then straightens and smiles and says hello back. "How are you doing? How's that neck?"

"Pretty good. I'm keeping it in line." Then you go shy and fumbling. "I heard that you've been unwell. How are you?"

"I'm fine now," he says, nodding. He does look fine, if you look at the surface of his face and don't know about the tumor, which must be gone now. His eyes look bright and clear. He has grown a goatee. No longer will he be the jet man in the razor ad. You think how good it is to see him. You talk about the abundance of cheap avocados—three for two dollars. There are new stalls at the market and now you can get crêpes and pies and beer. You mention the book he once recommended to you, *A New Earth* by Eckhart Tolle—which you'd thought was partly interesting and mostly silly, but which you say you liked. He's holding a canvas bag with bushels of celery sticking out the top. There is very little movement in his body. He stands quite stiffly with his head bowed toward your mouth. Then there's a quiet moment and the wind picks up as it always does, so you say, "Okay, well." He says it was good to see you and puts his hand on your shoulder. Then you each wander away to different stalls. You have a minor current of electricity buzzing on your shoulder from where he put his hand. You mindlessly spend the rest of your money on half a pumpkin and two kumara that are so large they look mutant; huge, dark gnarled things with frizzy antennae, they look like they should never have come up out of the ground. Now you have to eat them, and you've spent all your money. Your chiropractor floats into your head at odd moments during the next few weeks. Small, boring thoughts, like, I wonder what he made with the celery, and What is a tumor made of? But a few months later, when you go to see the new chiropractor to sort out your neck, which has seized up from too many hours sitting at your desk, she tells you, with mist in her kind eyes, that he has died. ⬙

Yusef Komunyakaa

from THE LAST BOHEMIAN OF AVENUE A

My friends keep stepping in front
of me, with prophet beards & bald
heads, saying, Let the dear crows
take me into the shadow of stone
before you, Rabbas. I let each one
cast his magic before shooing him
to the side, let each have his way
with the story, but I'm not brave.
When all the gone ones crowd
down by the river, calling me
by name & deeds, a young voice
will say to them, Boys & girls
at the end of the day I was born
of woman to play a mighty plea.

One evening, I ran into a dude
down on his luck
outside the Life Café,
humming "Willow Weep for Me."
I said, Here Bro, handing him
a balled-up twenty outta my boot,
& then returned to my dugout
to heat up a can of pork n beans.

Whatever it is, it hooks
up sweetly in the body,
you know. Whatever it is.
No wonder music in words
has taken me for a stroll
since I was seven, & my mind
always circles back like a hunk
of meat nagging on a shiny nail
pulled outta the cross
with a black crowbar.
A feeling grows outta the left
corner of an idea. But it isn't
random. No sir. It just is.
Like the night we're up there
slaying their demons,
& I'm surprised to hear
myself say, Guys, look,
we just laid down the first
track for our next LP,
"The Pearly Gates."
Lord, now here I am,
still troubling the water,
trying to honor everything

my brain takes in, going
from a mound of piano keys
to the naked homunculus
inside us, when the mind
wants only to eat light
as it faces stolen mercy.
But baby I don't have to
mumble in the dark to know
all I need to say to the night
is, Hold it right there
& don't move a muscle.

One night at the Vanguard
Max Bodenheim came up
to our table—the baroness
& me waiting for Thelonious
to sidle off the bandstand—
a little dance in his bones,
& I said, Can we help you?
He unfolds a few grubby pages,
& says, I don't think you can,
but maybe the lady can buy
this autographed masterpiece

for fifty cents—a dollar or two.
Something in his tone made me
ball both fists, & thank God
the baroness tugged my sleeve
& placed a dollar into his hand.
She took the poem-offering,
& he hurried to the bar
to buy a shot of whiskey.
I wanted to tell him the
flowers in snow & ice
didn't make any sense.
But a week later or so
I was totally stunned
when the baroness
handed me a copy of Max's
Naked on Ice Skates.
I almost forgave him
for thinking he was Valentino.
One day, he inched over to me
& said, I'm on the pottery wheel
every time you blow that tune.
We couldn't look each other
in the eye, but I tried not to shave

a number off his soul, & I said, Max,
I love women, & treat them
better than I treat myself,
& every day "Ruby, My Dear"
pours some life back into me.

Now the tune "Craving,"
I guess it's about searching
for evidence, to jab a hand
into a melon in a Georgia field,
searching for love. That tune
walked me to the tried edge,
& I stood gazing at my body
floating in a briny pool. But
as in dreams, I was in a room
with the girl down the street
lying nude in a king-size bed,
& Grandmamma downstairs
in that big clumsy brass bed
glad to breathe a last hymn.

Peaches sat on her back steps
gazing over at my bedroom
window, listening to me blow
soft as a wet sigh in the back
of the throat, or a crying sound
from some secret landscape.
Today, after fifty-some-odd
years, whenever I see Peaches,
she looks me dead in the eyes
& says, Why couldn't you hear
what I said to you years ago?
Her stepladder of six children
by six men crowns her as one
of those clay eaters, each child
individual as an Ornette solo.
I want to say to her, Peaches,
do you know where this horn
has taken me? I mean, yeah,
I could always see a hundred
angles & language in a tune.
Do you know what I'm trying
to say, where I've gone, Sister?
Roscoe, you don't remember

that August night in the park
because you weren't here yet,
even if things are now running
together, when it all should fit
into a shape of natural feeling.
I hardly know any of the faces
out there anymore, gazing up
with yes & no in their eyes,
as if I should be as alarmed
about black leather riot gear
for the movie. You've heard
the night cops had a field day
beating heads right across
my street, a parade of wild
drums captured on video,
as if hurting for the easiest
word to rhyme with homicide.
But I know something about
that infernal night I doubt
anyone else knows about,
& a clue is "Carolina Shout."

I can't think of a boxer
who can't dance,
not just a flat-footed
dynamo, his head
a punching bag
on a wobbly spinal hook.
Sooner & later the mouth
overloads, & a right jab
& left hook settles the score.
You gotta dance,
Rabbas, my grandpa
would say. Dance, boy!
Or, one of these days
you gonna crawl out
bloody from the sledge mill.
Twist & turn, then feint, light
as any prey on your feet,
then master an uppercut,
& you can boogie-woogie
the rest of your days, son.

I'd look at myself in the mirror
Victoria broke when she threw
her red shoes at me one Sunday
morning, & I've never been able
to put a whole man together
again, seeking my own love
for shadow play & infamy.

Rich People

Nobody stopped me. I smiled at the doormen like we were old friends. I followed the other guests and walked like I knew exactly where I had to be. The hallways were dim and reddish. Sometimes I made wrong turns and had to double back; even then I walked surely. As I got farther into the house there were more people about, and a deep humming pervaded the air. Some guests had hooks embedded in their necks and shoulders that trailed long graceful streamers. The flickering sconces made everybody look like stained-glass saints.

Abbey Mei Otis

Finally I reached the ballroom. Usually such places are a disappointment, but here the floor was a rink of gold. The walls soared up, the ceiling obscured by vapor and heat and candle smoke. Everywhere people stood and spoke to each other, their mouths bright clots of blood that slid around their faces. I moved through the crowd and caught flecks of conversation like insects in my hair.

"She's really opening herself up to the opportunity of this country," someone said.

"That submarine is just not a joy I want to live without any longer."

So this was the hum. It was as if they were putting on a show for me, though they were not. Even their most unguarded selves were a sumptuous performance. I felt awe.

Nearly every day I have passed by this house. I know its outside like a favorite picture book. The shards of glass embedded in the top of the garden wall, the gargoyles vomiting dirty water. I had always imagined what lay inside to be painted in colors that my eyes could not comprehend. Instead it felt as though I were descending deeper into my own brain. Anything I could think of existed somewhere in the ballroom. I saw a woman so laden with diamonds she had to bend over and crawl on all fours. The strands of diamonds hung down all around her body and over her head, making her look like a shaggy, sparkling dog.

A butler stepped into my vision, offering to squeeze truffle oil into my mouth from a dropper. I let it fall on my lips and then thought why the hell not; I kissed his meaty neck with reverence. Under his skin, his pulse deferred.

I rode a surge of blood or ocean. Imminently it would break upon the shore and I would learn something about myself. Seeking air I clicked across the golden floor, slipped through the glass doors and out onto the balcony. The night was sharp and alien. Many people mingled here as well, styling themselves explorers on a new planet. A woman lifted an ancient diving helmet off her head, shook out her long hair, and smiled to her companions. I went to the edge and looked over the railing. Glittering below was a fountain, a wide expanse of water in which many enormous fish, and also a small boy, had been turned to stone and now spat and pissed water elegantly through the air. Beyond the fountain was a severely curated lawn. Beyond the lawn someone had practiced the art of creating fragrant wilderness, vines and weeping trees that trembled in the breeze with desire. Beyond the trees I could see the lights of the city and the place I had come from.

A knot of people next to me laughed dangerously. One young man held a knife in his palm. Everyone backed away from him, licking their lips. He pinched the spine of the blade between his thumb and forefinger and flung the knife high up into the night. It vanished into the darkness, and he was so rich—everyone was so rich—that it never came down.

How rich were they? Here's how rich.

Rich enough that they could live forever and never be hurt by anything. Or else, rich enough that they could be hurt by everything and never need to worry. Some people there were even rich enough that they could slice off little bits of their own flesh and serve it to their friends on top of rice balls, like sushi. They nibbled each other, and then there were little gilt comment cards on which they rated their friends based on freshness and tenderness of flesh, superlative mouth-feel, choiceness of cut. I stood by the buffet tables and watched two people descend into a quarrel over the poor ratings they had given each other. They rolled their eyes and sneered, their lips still flavorful with the fat of the other.

> I saw a woman so laden with diamonds she had to bend over and crawl on all fours.

A tall man next to me laughed. "You see?" He rested the fingers of one hand on my elbow. "No friendship is so strong it cannot be destroyed by ratings."

I told him I didn't know what he meant at all. I asked him where were the foods that allowed you to forget everything in your life before the moment of biting down.

"That will take a long time," he said, and then he used some of his money to go talk to people more interesting than me.

At the other end of the buffet there was a table piled with whole roast chickens. Hundreds of them, bodies gleaming with crispy fat and smoke-infused salt and crackling herbs, stacked into a pyramid that towered over my head. The smell was nearly sexual.

There was an attendant nearby—who looked like every part of him was tucked into his pants—whose job was to ensure that when guests came to choose a chicken, they did not choose one from the bottom of the pyramid and cause all the rest to tumble down.

I went over to the table and the attendant helped me to select a hen from the top. "What will you name it?" he asked.

"Can I distinguish myself by refusing to give it a name?"

"No. Many people have already done that."

I named it Voltairine.

There were various pins you could affix to your chicken to make it unique. I chose two pins that looked like long-lashed eyes and stabbed them into my chicken's breast. People carried their chickens by inserting a fist into the body cavity and balancing it like a puppet on their arm. When they encountered another person with a chicken, they would both bobble the chickens around on their fists. They made different voices for their chickens, and had them converse about current events or philosophy or other scintillating subjects. Grease and herbs dripped from their elbows.

> Her face protruded right from the hollow of the tiger's throat, like a beautiful jewel or a second face.

A woman who had been ironed flat nudged her chicken coyly against mine. She had affixed a pair of bright red lips and a rainbow flag to her chicken. "But how can we possibly be enjoying ourselves when other people elsewhere are so sad?" her chicken asked mine.

I was flooded with terror that I would be found out, but I summoned strength to quell it and forced my chicken to speak. "Impossible pleasure is the only kind I want."

Her chicken laughed. "How of the now!"

My chicken understood then that there was nothing she could say that would distinguish her from the rich chickens. There was no belief she could espouse more extreme than the beliefs they could adopt for fashion. My breath came more quickly and I tried to remember why I had come here. The woman raised her chicken to my lips. "Would you like?"

Per etiquette, I took a big bite from the thigh. I raised my chicken and she took a bite in kind. The flesh was perfect, juicy, redolent with flavor. I ate more, trying to submerge my fear. We stood linked together in a circle, scraping with our teeth, ravenous, altered.

I don't know how people knew it was time to go outside. They swept me with them, down the grand staircase set with luminaries, out into the back garden. The fountain rippled in the moonlight. People thronged on the lawn. I swanned among them. Every part of me felt sated, dazed, and not only because I had eaten.

One of the things they enjoyed the most was slicing open the carcasses of animals and sliding inside them as though they were sleeping bags. On this beautiful half-moon of lawn, everybody was finally getting what they wanted. A man with a knife knelt in the grass and brought his blade through the belly of a dead tiger. His knife was a foot long and made of bone and it opened the tiger from throat to groin. His audience watched with eyes round enough to finally understand how good they had it. Her white belly fur looked so soft and deep, like you could sink into it, like maybe the knife had not punctured her flesh but only sunk into her fur. Of course there was all the blood, too.

There was a woman in a creamy dress with pearls seeded across her shoulders. It was her turn. She sat down in the grass next to the tiger and bent her knees. First she inserted her feet into the tiger. Then her calves, then her thighs. Then she lifted her butt so she could wiggle it inside. Someone near me made a small *oh* of either longing or grief. The lower part of the tiger carcass flipped around and you could tell the woman's feet were kind of cramped. Now she was entirely inside except for one arm, her shoulders, and her head. Based on her expression you couldn't tell what was happening to her. Something liquid and yellow-green was seeping through the pearls on her dress.

Now only her head was outside of the tiger. The knife man dropped the sheet of flesh he had been holding and made a joke motion as though he were zipping her up. Her face protruded right from the hollow of the tiger's throat, like a beautiful jewel or a second face.

From the side of the lawn people started pulling out the other animals they had already done. There was a walrus and a buffalo. There was a heartbreaking palomino horse. There was a reddish-gold bear big enough for two. People arranged them so they could be next to their friends. It became clear that everyone had buddies to sleep next to, while I had no one. I shrank back toward the aromatic trees.

"Wait!" A young woman with eyes like my own caught my wrist. "Please don't go." She pulled me with her across the lawn. "We can share!"

We spooned each other inside her elk. Every part of my body was swaddled with either elk flesh or the woman's body. Slick clumps slid between my fingers. Stringy bits dried on my neck.

"I made something for you." The young woman extracted one arm from the carcass and dangled a charm bracelet in front of my face. I couldn't grasp it and so it fell into my mouth. It tasted cool and coated with putrefaction.

I spat it out. "I can't take that."

"But I've never met anyone like you before."

She tried to pull my wrist up to fasten the bracelet around it and I elbowed her away. In struggling I rotated so I faced the young woman. She wiped blood from her eyes and mouth and then my eyes and mouth. Her face brimmed with kindness. "I think we could be friends."

The way she said it I knew it was true. We would never be bound by necessity, only inclination. I had never been given such a gift before. I could go home with her if I wanted. I could tell her what I had done and we could eat wild mushrooms fried in butter and absolve each other with friendship.

Either that notion or the stench of raw flesh was heady and I thought I would rupture.

"That's not what I want!"

I tried to push myself out of the sleeping bag, but I was so slippery I could not get purchase on anything. As I flailed it occurred to me that whether I accepted her or refused her, I could not hold myself apart. Why had I feared discovery? There was nothing to discover. Simply by reaching for power, I attained it. Simply by walking in, I became one of them.

She began to reminisce about our long acquaintance, how as children we rode a polo pony into the pool and it tried to drag itself up the ladder by its teeth before drowning. She was so rich the stories came true as she spoke them. My tears mingled with the viscera that pillowed my head. But I had thought I was choosing; just once, I had wanted to be a person who could choose.

The young woman hummed a familiar lullaby in my ear. The elk flesh held me as tightly as it had held the insides of the elk. Eventually I stopped shuddering. All around me people murmured to each other and wriggled reverently in their sleeping bags. Light fell down from the sky and brushed our faces with silver. Tomorrow we would rise from these skins and do everything we wanted. The sleepover had begun. 🛡

Shane McCrae

LINES COMPOSED AT 34 NORTH PARK STREET, ON CERTAIN MEMORIES OF MY WHITE GRANDMOTHER WHO LOVED ME AND HATED BLACK PEOPLE LIKE MYSELF. JULY 15, 2017

America I was I think I was

Seven I think or anyway I prob-

ably was   nine   I anyway was nine

And riding in the back   seat of our tan

Datsun 210   which by the way Amer-

ica I can't believe   Datsun is just

Gone   anyway   America I was

Riding in the back   seat we were we my grand-

mother and I were passing the it must

Have been a mall   but I have tried   and can't

Remember any malls in Austin at

The time America but do I really

Remember Austin really   I remember

This thing that happened   once when I was passing

A mall in Austin so   the mall so Austin

But then and when America will my

Grandmother be   my memories of her her-

self be replaced by memories of just

Her presence near   important or unusu-

al things that happened does that happen will

That happen we   America we were

Anyway passing   on a city street

But next to it the   mall and actually

I might have been in the front seat actually

And maybe it was   winter all the windows

Were rolled up maybe or at least the one

Right next to me   in the front seat Amer-

ica when for   no reason I could see the

Window exploded   glass swallowed me   the way

A cloudburst swallows a car   glass and a

Great stillness   flying glass and stillness both

Together   then the stillness left   and I

Jumped either over my   seat or between

The seats   into the back America

Or neither   here I might just be remem-

bering the one real accident I've ever

Been in I was   a child still maybe seven

Or nine and we   were in an intersec-

tion hit   and I for sure jumped then my grand-

mother and I again already my

Memories of the Datsun breaking seem

More solid than my memories of her

America   but I remember her

Mobile home filling up with trash   until

She couldn't walk through any room   and still she

Walked through her rooms she walked the way I walk

Through stores   suspicious   and aloof watched e-

ven by the products I consume consumed

By you America   O cloud of glass

Adam Clay

A JOKE ABOUT HOW OLD WE'VE BECOME

I take a break from one thought or another
to pay a credit card bill,
to take the dog out, to water the two

plants in the hanging basket
because Kim asked me to,
but why not instead take a walk

through the early August morning
before the heat wave hits
while the body still stretches itself out?

The music goes from minor to major
when you flip the album, but sometimes
the minor starts over before you

cross the room (it's a big room)
and sometimes it's best to just listen,
it's best to not fill any space with words

but the stars and the stripes catch
the eye more so than the white
blank space like a life to be filled up with

something bigger than itself. My dad
last night on the phone telling me the tests
came back positive but not to worry (but how

not to worry?), his almost three decades
ahead of me and what is a year
really when they pile up, time to dust

the furniture again, to check
on the sink that's draining slow,
clean it out, start the day with a list

of what a day should even mean
or be, not minding how fast the hours go by
until I will mind, which by then it will

be too late, though I do not mean
my life means anything in the scheme
of stepping back we all do, chipping

at some unmovable block of rock
as if time won't eventually
undo even its looming shape too.

Berlin Dispatches to Remember Me By

J. Jezewska Stevens

A VISIT

Today the phone rang—twice. I did not pick up. I tend to avoid the phone, I think. Maybe even more than I avoid people. Though in the end it's hard to say which element of the conversation I detest more, the phone or the people who call. If I had to guess, I would say the phone. Or maybe it's the people? It's true that when the phone rang just now, I was afraid to see who it was. To see the identity of the avoided flit across the screen only brings on a worse kind of guilt, I find, when still I ignore the call. Which is why out here, on the narrow veranda, abreast the basil plant, I simply pretend I do not hear it when, for the third time now, the receiver registers a ring. I stay right where I am, enjoying an uninterrupted spell of ignorance. Then I hear a yell from the street. The voices are low, a little abashed. That is my name, I think, that's being shouted! Once, twice. I pause. I notch the cigarette into a groove in the tray. Then I peer over the balcony edge, around the fragrant basil plant, just in time to see the backs of the heads of two very dear friends of mine, friends who are even dearer to each other than they are to me—they have been engaged for years, the wedding keeps getting delayed—disappear around the *Spätkauf* at the end of the block. That is the sound barrier of my own voice, I discover: the length of a block. I wave. Back home, on Eighth Avenue, it's likely my voice would have carried one and a half blocks, even two. Necessary adjustments will have to be made. Here people are gone, indifferent to you in the time it takes to walk to the end of a single block, not one and a half, not two. And to think we might have shared a cigarette—! Really, I don't know why I didn't answer when they called.

What if it had been you?

J. JEZEWSKA STEVENS

A CUP OF LIPTON

The oldest tea shop in the neighborhood really isn't very old at all, established as it was in 1991. I go once a week. The shop carries jasmine in the grades of fancy, very fancy, flowering pearl, and deluxe. You can imagine which one I always buy. But today, when I come home with my small paper bag, folded over at the top and stapled just so, I am struck with acute regret. It seems to me some exquisite happiness has passed me by, or else remained stationary, like a ripe bud ready to pluck, back in the musk of the shop. It must be said: I am disappointed with my regular fancy tea. The sun slants through my window and through the windows of the apartments below, and I wonder how many people around me, in this very same sunbeam, on this very same block, on Maybachufer Straße, are currently preparing for themselves the very fancy, flowering pearl, or deluxe. The tea sets of my mind proliferate on delicate trays with golden handles and friezes, and, like a woman eavesdropping on a party from which she was excluded—and indeed

> It must be said: I am disappointed with my regular fancy tea.

this is exactly the case—I look on with deepening resentment as the superior jasmine steeps. Of course, there was little to stop *me* from purchasing the deluxe, the very fancy, or the dull green and flowering pearls, with the caveat that these varieties come at double or even triple the price of the regular fancy tea. Still, I might have bought one of these superior strains, only less of it, and so remained well within my tea budget for the week. But it isn't the same, to buy less than you'd like. To come home with an eighth of a pound instead of a quarter. Better to hold in the palm the full weight of the regular fancy grade that I have chosen. A quarter pound will last me through this Wednesday, at least, at which point I will even begin to look forward to my Lipton, into whose imitative arms I'll turn, come Thursday, once the jasmine has run out. A cup of Lipton will get you through the day. And it can be nice to have the sachet, I find, once the tea is drunk. The dregs find a second life in soothing a blemish or reducing puffiness around the eyes. Although, one ought to take precautions. Once, when I was trying to make a blemish disappear, I left on my forehead a rather too saturated sachet for rather too long—perhaps I even dozed off—and later, when it was time to go to meet a date for dinner, I found I'd acquired a dark stain above my eye that no amount of soap could mute. It was a bruise-like stain that lasted for days. It drew attention to my head. The date, by the way, went very well. The man I met was charmed and made copious eye contact—or perhaps he was only staring at my Lipton bruise. I have to ask, he said. What is this on your face? He reached across the hen carcasses that languished on the table. I love it, he said. I can't stop looking at you. He thought the stain was the most wonderful thing about me, for a few hours he may have even fallen in love, and what would you have done, in my position? How could I have possibly told him it was only a temporary mark, that in fact I was not so unique or deluxe as he imagined me to be? And indeed his enthusiasm has begun to wane. It was fading by the second date or maybe the third, once the stain had vanished, and I was drinking fancy jasmine, instead of Lipton, and looking quite myself again.

> He thought the stain was the most wonderful thing about me.

RE: RULES
In a book I adore a woman writes:
  1. *Do not write more than once per month.*
  2. *Never mention the past.*

A LOOPHOLE
Perhaps I will write to you every day and collate my dispatches into one.

SPIELPLATZ
It is astonishing, really, the extent to which the twins are not the same. The little boy chases a ball across the park, a streak of red delight. Later he runs his fingers through my hair and tells me really, I must wash. Things are not so easy with the little *Fräulein*. She is uncanny, like a cat. Her watchful eyes. Today she installs herself in the window with a slice of toast and jam and asks, Is it better to take one good bite with all the jam at once, or spread it evenly so every bite has just a little bit? Girls are much too prone to tragedy, I find. They seem to know it intuitively: something is wrong with the toast. And then they ask and ask, like pressing on a bruise. *Liebling*, I say. You can always have more jam.

A PARTY
I am getting along with my mother better than I have in ages now that we are communicating across several thousand miles, via the phone. We talk about gardens. We talk about food. She wants to know, What are you

eating over there? What did you have for lunch? Recently I called to ask for the chocolate sheet cake recipe she used to make on birthdays. Cocoa. Flour. Butter. Sugar. And cinnamon, my mother said. Cinnamon—the one thing everyone forgets. I didn't forget. I went out to the store and bought each item in the appropriate amount, including the vial of *Zimt*. It's still there, actually, among the other groceries, in the bag on a hook in the hall. It hasn't moved a bit. I suppose by the time I came home from the store I'd lost the heart to bake a cake. The will withered within me, like an old fruit. In the kitchen there wasn't a measuring cup or tablespoon to be found, only a scale that measures out ingredients in grams. And it had been quite enough to produce the translations—cinnamon to *Zimt*, sugar to *Zucker*, chocolate to *Schokolade*—without converting the called-for quantities from imperial to metric as well. I took a deep breath. I stared at the scale. Then I retreated here to the veranda to keep company with the really luscious basil plant my *Mitbewohnerin* tends, and which seems to have grown ever more alive, ever fuller, in the time since I arrived, no matter how much ash—whole grams of it, I expect—I tamp into the soil. But I wouldn't know. Such matters are beyond me, in the end. This business of grams and cups and kilojoules, the density of basil leaves, the timer on the phone that logs the minutes I spend speaking to my mother. Did you make the cake? she asks, as we approach minute twenty-two or -three. Another day, I say. Tomorrow, I say. The party is tomorrow. Or maybe it was today? There's a thought. Perhaps that's why my dear, almost-married friends just called.

RE: SYLVIA

How stylish to finish work at two o'clock and join the party then, at just the hour when the crowd, like a too-warm drink, is in need of freshening. And on top of this to pay the rent? Really, she sounds grand. It makes me wonder if perhaps I should have been a waitress. How different things would be. Oh, to be forever fashionably late, to have always some new story of rich couples fumbling with forks, and cash from tips on hand. Let me be the first to tell you: No one in Germany is fashionably late, not even I. I wait with diligence at crosswalks here, one little Schumacher twin dangling from either wrist. In Berlin the signals sound aloud to usher the blind.

AN ARABIAN NIGHT

My *Mitbewohnerin* keeps plenty of different kinds of things to eat stored in the little armoire in the kitchen. I admire the variety. I often lift the latch and take a peek, just to see how things are coming along. On her shelf, I find the strange still life of two apples, a bag of yellow egg noodles to off-set the beefy burgundy of stroganoff, and also a half loaf of bread. The Germans are really very proud of their bread. Also their egg noodles, if I'm not mistaken. Certainly I can see putting forth *these* egg noodles as an object of national pride. The blue seal is brand-new and the noodles are perfectly shaped into soft-edged waves, as if shaved away in short, small strokes from a block of waxy dough. If it were up to me, I would walk to the *Supermarkt* this instant to buy such a package of egg noodles for myself. Only, it isn't up to me. On evenings like these, everyone is out by the Spree drinking pilsner straight from the bottle, and that includes the person-nel from the *Supermarkt*. Automatic belts convey name-brand egg noodles onto the scales of my mind. Of course I support the early closing of the shops. I think everyone ought to have a day of rest. The only trouble is, my inner clock is still set to Eighth Avenue time, according to which the hour for grocery shopping falls well past ten. It is a problem of profound jet lag. Here, during the actionable hours of the day, I go for a walk. I open a book. I slip the bookmark from my copy of *Arabian Nights* with the idea of read-ing through to the end of a chapter, the denouement, only to find that the story goes on and on, I am once more transported to some new world, the tales are tucked one within the other and always beginning again. Later, I think, I will go the store. After dinner, I think. I turn the page. Now the time for dinner has come and gone, and out the window I can see the dark and velvet sky. Perhaps I should go to have a beer myself. There's a solu-tion. Pretzels and *Bier*. Then I really would be edging down the slippery slope to becoming Deutsche.

A SALE

It's no picnic biking home with two kilos of *Schoko Müsli*, I'll admit. Put two kilos of anything in the basket of a bike and things can get topsy-turvy. But I made it home, however inelegantly, and for a brief and glorious time this apartment contained so much *Schoko Müsli* that I thought I would never run out. Take a long look at two kilos of any breakfast food and you will see what I mean. For days I lived under the assumption that there was enough *Müsli* here to hold me over until December or into next spring, when my visa will expire. I thought perhaps I'd bring some home for you to try. But in the end *Schoko Müsli* is no different from water or crude oil or any other resource drawn from kitchen pantries or the bosom of the earth.

Life is hemmed in by scarcity on every front, I am reminded, once the *Schoko Müsli* finally runs out. Probably it's for the best. Probably I would have gotten bored of *Schoko Müsli*, in the end. I wonder sometimes, Will you too get bored? I pose this question to the basil plant. It wilts a little, absorbs more ash.

QUESTIONS

What happens, for example, if one dies over here while on an au pair's visa? Do they ship your body back across the pond? And how much does that cost? Who pays? Who is morally responsible for those transactions that slip through the wide weave of the neoliberal net? Can you ship a body collect? Is that what socialism is, the power of attorney to ship a corpse on the taxpayer's dime? How will I go? When will I go? Will it be in Tiergarten, on a bike, after spilling groceries to the path? Or in the Spree, caught in the paddle wheel of a tourist pontoon? What will they tell you? Who will tell you? What will they tell the twins?

> **Life is hemmed in by scarcity on every front, I am reminded, once the *Schoko Müsli* finally runs out.**

A FREDDIE CIGARETTE

After a panic a cigarette can be nice, and the best kind to have is a Freddie. The only trouble is, Freddies can be very difficult to find. They are French, if I recall. Perhaps that's why. In France I imagine Freddies are thrown about fast and loose and sold on the cheap, but Berlin sings a different tune. Today, a trip to the *Spätkauf* yields only further pocketfuls of Camel Blues. Come to think of it, I don't believe I've ever managed to procure a pack of Freddies on my own. I must have been quite dependent on a friend of mine who departed all those months ago, back when I was still smoking Freddies. He always had a pack on hand. He had very strong opinions about very small things, like the best brand of cigarettes, or whether summer rolls count as a lunch or a snack, and it's possible his opinions influenced mine as we smoked there on the banks of the Spree, passing Freddies back and forth. From time to time the current pulled a pontoon of tourists into view, and the tourists on board would wave. Once, my friend lifted a hand in response—the one holding a Freddie—and, as if on command, some cheeky flaneur on the upper deck bent against the rail and raised, into the late summer dusk, the high white moon of his ass. It was radiant, as I recall. Things like this happen, you see, when you are smoking Freddies. The whole world is more radiant with a Freddie in hand.

RE: BREAKFAST

I eat oatmeal for breakfast every morning here while living in Berlin. It is really quite a production. Sometimes, right in the middle of a batch, one must add more water. Other times, more oats. I like to think I have a knack. Once, when I was taking language classes at the library, I came right out with it: *Ich koche den besten Müsli gern!* It was, of course, a glancing truth, a slightly coded reveal. For *Müsli* is not quite the same as oatmeal, in the end, although it is indeed related—I wouldn't turn up my nose, for example, at a pot in which oatmeal and *Müsli* mingled. But at the time the question was posed to me, *Was kochst du gern?*, I did not know the word for oatmeal as it is ordered—if it is ever ordered—here in the cafés of Berlin. Perhaps in some later unit one encounters the words for anglophone and Asian foods, like "oatmeal" or "moon cake." Perhaps someday I'll go back and learn. For now, I have stopped attending. I simply couldn't keep up. What do you do? Where are you from? What will you become? these strangers rudely asked. And it would seem the future tense is not for me. Here I am, fixed firmly in the present of a noonday kitchenette, clinging to the lower rungs of human knowledge. More milk? More water? Are the berries warm?

> From Saturn's rings, however, the Earth is adorable. An ornamental button fallen from some stylish coat.

UNEMPLOYMENT

Who could have ever imagined I'd come to miss the Schumacher twins? All that snot. All those playdates. And now—all this extra time.

LATVIA

Recently people have been speaking to me most frequently in French. *Parlez vous—?* they say, and I am forced to shake my head. *Nein.* Not French? Not German? What are you, then? So they say. The other day, at the bike repair shop, someone posed this question of national origin only to answer it himself: You are from Latvia, he said. I answered that, to the best of my knowledge, this was not the case. A pause. A brow befuddled. I could have sworn that you are Latvian, said the German man. I was so sure that he was wrong. But this was weeks ago, and things are different now. Now, standing here before my *Mitbewohnerin*'s armoire, considering a little can of easy-open peanuts whose lid releases with a *pfft*, even I have come to doubt where I am from. Here in the dark, bracketed by the open armoire doors, I feel I could be from anywhere, it wouldn't make any difference at all. And perhaps I owe this rootless mood to the country my passport says I'm from, a nation forever staring into other people's pantries, reaching in an arm.

NEWS

Today astronomers have released a photograph of Earth taken from very far away. From the rings of Saturn, actually. They sweep through the upper half of the frame, a vast tan curve against the cold obsidian of space. The Earth, meanwhile, isn't how I remember it at all. It is reduced to a round blue bead, harmless and pristine, whereas up close, when photographed from the vantage of the moon, for example, it has always struck me as menacing and grave. From Saturn's rings, however, the Earth is adorable. An ornamental button fallen from some stylish coat. One hardly feels sorry for it. The real object of sympathy, in the end, is the sacrificial satellite, sent out on a thirteen-year journey from which it will never return. Soon, I read, it will dive down to the dissipated surface of the planet at incinerating speeds, and so be reduced to dust. I wonder: Why not settle for the rings?

RE: INTERVIEW

You write that you, too, are thinking of moving away. Please don't. You are so wonderful as and where you are. How am I to imagine you in some new and unknown place, walking briskly by a strip of unfamiliar shops? Eighth Avenue suits us, didn't you know, in the photo albums of my mind. But how nice for you. Good luck.

Forgive me my contrarian streak, but I have to disagree with Sylvia. Obviously you should wear the slacks and navy blouse.

A MANDARIN ORANGE

I have become the kind of person whose nose is always running. The kind of person I always dreaded becoming—now the day has arrived. She has snuck up on me, this jaded woman, who is so sniffly, especially when she eats or walks too quickly in the cold, and the heels of whose socks have worn away, and whose pants never fit quite right. Yesterday, when I went out for a new pair of trousers, determined to reverse this unfortunate regress, I found that nothing I tried made me look quite as nice as the mannequins hanging from hooks in the Türkischer Markt. One pair was too loose in the legs and snug in the hips, another tight in the calves and roomy in the waist. I stood before the mirror and wondered what kind of woman the manufacturer could possibly have had in mind. Not me, in any case. I left the store without buying any pants at all. Though if I'd had to choose, were it a choice between one of those two pairs and walking half-naked out onto the street, I would without question have chosen the pair too loose in the legs. It is almost impossible, in my opinion, to find a pair of pants that is *too* loose in the legs. It is as much a matter of comfort as self-defense. I like to feel I have the necessary range of motion to dash away in the event of some unexpected threat—and the worst kinds of threats are always unexpected, one must always be prepared to dash away. Although, dashing down the street, especially in autumn, is yet another activity that tends to make my nose run so unattractively. It interferes with the breath. It seems to me a nervous habit, an anxious byproduct of simply being alive. I genuinely hoped it would never come to this. That the very fact of living would so constantly remind me of my death. That it does makes me quite depressed. I suppose one cannot dash away from oneself, in the end. What I need is something light and cheerful—a floral skirt, not pants. A patch of sun, not lying supine in the dark. I slip a Kleenex into the pocket of the skirt, apply a shock of lipstick to my lips. Then I saunter out to the store in search of some ten-cent solution, which arrives, would you believe it, in the form of a mandarin orange. 🜨

HALO

On the X-ray I could see the fracture,
the shadow veining through the ghost
of the vertebra he cracked playing
football, hard-nosed in the driveway
because it was Sunday, and Sunday
means church and football in America,
even if you are Yaqui. And because
he was Yaqui he played and prayed
to the tattoo of Santa Teresa scrolled
up his forearm. And because my job,
the legal guardian of the group home,
had the power over matters his
—school, work, body—I signed for
the halo brace they screwed into his skull,
one needle at a time to deaden nerves,
one pin at a time to restrict mobility,
each entering a dissent I cringed with.
And because white and educated
sort-of, I qualified to hold his hand
across the threshold of each turn
the wrench made, each tear not shed
because never cry in front of a white man.
And I held his hand, the one that killed

a man in Tucson in a fight he didn't ask for,
but killed the man anyway, with a knife
in the street, a detail I knew but forgot
as I forgot all the crimes of those kids
my boss called my *charges*, because
I could, and forgetting is privilege.
The way I forgot to tell the boss I too
had a record, a fact I quietly expunged,
because whiteness affords slippage.
Lord knows, nothing bespeaks the redress
of genocide and systemic brutality
like sending a white boy from Jersey
to tighten a spiral, to close the loop
in his cursive, a kid not much older
than the one gripping my hand because
I was there, on duty, because he asked me
to stay with him when they set the halo in
like an angel I said, *like a deer head*
he said, because Pascua Yaqui dancers
strap the heads of deer to their own
heads, because Sonora, because Yaqui,
and the heads of deer and heads of Yaqui

are *not like* but *of*. And because the border
of the reservation is white on one side,
rez on the other, they promised no pain,
they promised fear and fixed his head
to see only forward as if pinning him
to the ground to stare at an eclipse.
And because I am no tourist to suffering,
I gave no tears. And because he asked,
and the landscape of feeling is my song,
I waited for him to fade into the midday
night of codeine. Then wept, wept white,
in the corridor, the parking lot, looping
into a gray cloud as I drove back home
to other kids, who said nothing about
the ghost I was wearing on my face,
the song I hardly deserve to call my own,
if it is mine or his, this house, this country,
wherever we are, we have come to.

THIS DRINK TASTES LIKE HISTORY

April, Richmond, a scattering of blossoms,
horse chestnuts over the Confederate lawn

like a memory of snow, and the bloom-gone
tweeking limbs shot thin as charcoal drawings of

one-way junkies stepping off a Greyhound—
I imagine Levis thinking something like that,

Etch-A-Sketching in his mind as the bartender
at the Hill Café pours a round just after noon.

His body a hotel crammed from long strung-out
toomuchness, edgy in the purgatory of a score,

he is smirking warmly at stray grad students
sorting futures on beer naps. Nowhere near 1996

it is now, and now is irrecoverable as a wave,
as this drink, which sends me into history,

then a field outside a barn gig to empty out
under stars. The band's covering Bowie,

so in my head I am eleven, skinny, boardwalk
strutting along the Steel Pier in Atlantic City.

High above on a platform, a woman wearing
a swimsuit and football helmet sits bareback

on a horse, waiting to coax the unnatural into real.
The first "Diving Girl" was named Sonora.

She went blind from hitting the water wrong
and kept diving another eleven years. That's why

this one is wearing aviator goggles. That the helmet's
leather, no face mask, the kind my father wore

playing noseguard, is a detail that indicts the detailer.
Yes, it's a good day to muck around the mid-1970s,

my father standing beside me, a relic—polo shirt,
buzz cut, most of his teeth lost to a field of men,

sweating *manhattans, whiskey sours.* A good
drinker, almost everyone loved his commitment,

not my mother, who just leapt out of the marriage;
which, if this were a script, you would already know.

The idea of Atlantic City was to become dream,
aspire toward another world, the way, in a field—

Levis and my father alive, hovering, I disappear
in the wake of my breathing. It works a bit, a spell,

a hit off a pipe in a dive bathroom. In the end
the woman and horse land in a pool and my father

says, *Now that's a broad.* In the end my father
wasted his material. I am now the age he was then,

the age Levis was in '96 and the man who tended
bar at the Hill Café is the same man serving drinks.

Small world. And symmetry being occasion,
but I get confused speaking across decades.

They drift into each other, snow across a road.
Remember the snow? Reader, can I call you Reader?

Have we hung enough we can let go formalities
of distance? Did you skid home, get snowed in, like me,

with a woman whose voice could fill and sink you,
your chest the walls of a low house in a floodplain?

When she sang it felt like a first listening,
like she was returning it to purity. Days later,

the plow showed, and she became a painting,
a landscape she invited me to walk out of.

Or maybe I simply bored her and she left.
Sometimes I hear her on the radio and think snow

then *blessed*. One storm, slow-mo spectacle.
All this happened in 1996. Impossible: my father,

a woman I knew through accident of weather,
and Levis fidgeting, politely enduring company.

And just when they dissolve into each other,
Levis leans across the bar of this dream and says:

You are telling this for a reason. And maybe
you should stop turning women into paintings.

Some nights my life unspools like cans of 8 mm
film spilling off the shelf of the sky, and I am

making it here in the dark, hands and a story
of hands, trying the buttons of my trousers

in a field where I leave the whole shit show,
and let the field resolve to be itself, the blank

screen at the end of the reel. And once I am
almost gone, what love becomes emptiness?

Walking away, calling back—Low whistle,
recurring wind, snow shifting across a road,

a song the band's way inside, another round.
White, the horse was white, a mare; as in

monster, foolish woman, the sea. Depending
on what you mean, somehow it matters.

The Grand
Claremont Hotel

Catherine Lacey

for Jesse Ball

AS THE RESULT OF A CLERICAL ERROR, OR WHAT SEEMED TO BE
a clerical error, I lived in room 807, an Economy Queen, on the eighth
floor of the Grand Claremont Hotel, free of charge, for nineteen days.

As I was returning to the hotel on the final evening of my original res-
ervation, a five-night business trip I had undertaken on behalf of The
Company, the desk attendant handed me a pale beige envelope made of
exquisite, heavy paper, paper of such a high quality, such weight, that one
might feel—whether correctly or incorrectly—that even by holding such
an object one's life had just been irrevocably changed. The envelope had
a matte navy lining and contained a thick note card embossed with the
Grand Claremont Hotel's official logo—a small illustration of the Grand
Claremont Hotel's façade, encircled by ornate typography reading: *The
Grand Claremont Hotel*.

In dark blue ink and intricate calligraphy, the note card read:

> *Due to Client Complaints*
> *The Company has no choice*
> *but to cease your employment.*

I stood in the lobby, briefcase at my feet, and read the note card several
times, studying the tiny variations between each capital C—this loop a lit-
tle wider, this one a little more narrow—counting and recounting the syl-
lables—it failed to be a haiku—and I wondered whether the speaker of
this message had indicated which words were to be capitalized or whether
the calligrapher had made such a decision on their own.

Stowing the note card and envelope in my overcoat's interior pocket, I thanked the desk attendant, took the elevator to the eighth floor, walked slowly to room 807, hung the *Do Not Disturb* sign on the exterior door handle, ingested a quantity of liquid from the minibar, and tucked myself into bed.

As I fell asleep—and I have always been an excellent sleeper, rarely if ever kept awake by fear or worry—I had a very clear realization that, in all likelihood, I would never again enter Company Headquarters, a building I had spent much time entering, exiting, and being inside. Indeed, each day of my life for the past twelve years had been defined by the hour I was expected to enter Company Headquarters, how long I would need to remain within Company Headquarters, the tasks I would need to complete that day at Company Headquarters, and the hour at which I could reasonably permit myself to exit Company Headquarters. On the days I was not expected to enter Company Headquarters, I was often abroad, meeting with clients on behalf of The Company. Upon completing these meetings, I had always returned to Company Headquarters to give reports on my travels, but now I had been informed that this pattern would go on no longer. What daily activities, I wondered, if anything, could replace my entrances and exits of Company Headquarters, my service to The Company, the way in which The Company directed and used the hours of my life?

I stood in the lobby, briefcase at my feet, and read the note card several times, counting and recounting the syllables— it failed to be a haiku.

In my twelve years of employment at The Company, I had known other men who had been informed their labor was no longer needed by The Company.

Few had met this news peacefully.

One, some years ago, had cried out expletives and something about a sick wife that could be heard all over Company Headquarters before he was escorted from the building and never heard from again. Another had jumped off the roof of Company Headquarters—though, the building isn't tall enough to cause significant damage, so he'd ended up only crushing both his legs. Another had simply gone home, gone to sleep, and never woken up.

And now, wrapped in high thread count sheets and blankets, the use of which had been paid for by The Company, I had become one of these men for whom The Company had no use. This fact seemed to transfigure into a physical mass or a kind of pressure in room 807; I became aware of the subtle but undeniable sensation that I was being watched, as if my dismissal had been transfigured into an actual human being who stared at me as I fell asleep. Yet I also knew I was not being watched, that I was completely alone in the sumptuous folds of the Grand Claremont Hotel's luxury bedding. The mattress sucked me into itself in a way that was not at all reminiscent of my simple cot back at home, in the bare apartment I'd long kept for its affordable rate and proximity to Company Headquarters. I fell asleep with a perverse sense of comfort.

I awoke quite late the next morning. Light slipped in at an angle. The curtain fluttered above an air vent.

I sat up in bed, propped a pillow between my back and the wall-mounted headboard. On the side table there was a navy rotary phone, a lamp with a pleated, navy shade, a Grand Claremont Hotel notepad and matching ballpoint pen with navy lettering along the shaft: *The Grand Claremont Hotel*. By the small window was a small chair. The walls were covered in thatched beige wallpaper.

I loved room 807. I respected room 807's implacable room-ness.

I lifted the phone, dialed room service, ordered the Grand Claremont Club Sandwich with a side of fruit salad. The sandwich arrived a half hour later accompanied by a dill pickle spear unmentioned by the menu. I consumed this meal in bed, in full, in silence.

I felt there was just no reason to leave room 807. I appreciated its beige-and-navy color scheme, its reassuring blankness. It was effective at its task—to be a room in which one could exist, gathering smells and washing them away, becoming weary and sleeping and becoming awake and becoming weary again. The four-foot-by-four-foot shower collected nearly an inch of standing water and though I realize this may be considered to be a plumbing defect, I appreciated this defectiveness as the shower's puddle gently softened the soles of my feet. The sink fixtures and cabinet pulls were ergonomic. The lighting was efficient and unromantic. Room 807 was remarkably unremarkable and yet I found so much in room 807 to remark upon, a paradox that amused me greatly, made me feel as if I had a deeply entwined understanding of room 807, as if room 807 and

I were devoted siblings sharing a sly glance during Christmas breakfast as our father told some well-worn boyhood story that became more epic with each telling. We were irrefutably enmeshed. I loved room 807. I respected room 807's implacable room-ness. No one could ever take the job of being a room away from this room, my dear room 807. I had no intrinsic motivation or desire to leave room 807, and if I ever did leave room 807, I realized, this would only be the result of someone else's insistence. I waited for the gentle knock of a housekeeper, perhaps a phone call warmly reminding me of the check-out policy, some kind of signal that the final moment of my stay at the Grand Claremont Hotel had come and my departure was, unfortunately, required and would also be greatly appreciated.

But there was no knock or call.

For three days I did not leave room 807, nor did I call room service, nor did I move unless absolutely necessary. I left the *Do Not Disturb* sign on the exterior doorknob and the sign did its job faithfully, guarding me from any manner of disturbance. Most of the time I lay in the stupefying and slightly perfumed bed. I felt beautifully empty, nothing more than a life. If I noticed a hunger or thirst, I consumed a cashew nut, a candied fruit, a gulp of faucet water. This is how I lived. This is what I became. At some point I even ceased to be waiting for a knock or call. I forgot what sound was.

On the third day, rested but somehow restless, I began to move the chair from its place by the window, into the bathroom, back to the window, to the bathroom, and back to the window, a gentle labor, something to get through. I covered the television set with a sheet and placed the phone beneath the bed and moved the chair between window and bathroom until night, then tucked the chair into bed with me. We had been through so much. I slept very well. So did the chair.

Late in the afternoon of my fourth day in room 807, I put my Grand Claremont Hotel bathrobe over my regular clothes, opened the door, walked down the hallway, filled my ice canister at the automated machine, made brief eye contact through an open doorway with a maid as she snapped a white sheet open above a queen bed identical to mine, then I returned to room 807. I stood at the door, seething with joy, ecstatic in my solitude and ecstatic for the solitude of others, far from or near to me, contained in their other rooms, in their beds, in their bodies.

It was only four in the afternoon but I had a dry vermouth on ice, the last item from the minibar. I fell asleep quickly but awoke two hours later feeling bolder, as if I had just been reconstituted after some kind of total disintegration. I opened my door, removed the *Do Not Disturb* sign, and shut the door. I called room service and had them send up the Grand Claremont Steak Dinner Deluxe and a whole bottle of barley wine and that night I feasted with all the lights on, the curtains drawn back. I watched the people of that city stroll the streets below me, move around in the windows of neighboring buildings, and I felt I was almost speaking to all these people, enduring beside them as all our lives ticked by. I waved at some of them but none saw my wave, yet I believed they felt it. Yes, I believed it was felt.

The next morning the ecstasy of my ice-machine journey and meal and revelation had faded. I was staring into the mirror just for the company when I heard several short door knocks and the word *housekeeping*, spoken in such a way you could almost call it singing. I went to the door, opened it, and found the same maid I had seen in that other room. She was considerably shorter than me but obviously more powerful and efficient, the sort of person who could paint a whole room without spilling a drip or taping the trim. Beside the maid was a rolling cart tidily stocked with cleaners and tight stacks of sheets and towels.

We smiled at each other, I think. At least she smiled. We remained still. After some time I remembered what this was all about, that this was the disturbance that I had allowed when I had revoked my door handle order to not be disturbed. The maid was the disturbance of sudden order.

Leaving the door open, I walked across the room, took a seat in the chair beside the window, and watched the city as she went about her business. It seemed only a few minutes had passed when I heard the maid say, *All done goodbye*, in one breath, the door shutting behind her. I turned to see room 807 made taut—my suitcase had been moved to the closet and the sheet had been removed from the television set and the telephone returned to its place beside the bed. It was as if I had never been there. I felt like an entirely new person in an entirely new room. I fell asleep that night in the chair. The room remained pristine.

On the nineteenth day there was a knock at the door. It was a slow, heavy knock—not the rapid tapping of a maid passing by—a knock followed by a baritone voice projected through the door—*I'm so sorry to be a bother, but may we speak for a moment?*

There had been, I was told, a gross oversight on the part of the bookings department and I would need to vacate room 807 immediately. The man who told me this was wearing an immaculately tailored suit the same reassuring shade of navy consistent among all Grand Claremont Hotel paraphernalia. Everyone here at the Grand Claremont Hotel, I was told, was deeply sorry for this inconvenience, and they all sincerely hoped that I could forgive them, however an Exclusive King Room on the twentieth floor was ready for my occupancy.

I thought of telling him that it was really quite all right, that I should be moving along anyway, that perhaps nineteen days in the Grand Claremont Hotel was enough days in the Grand Claremont Hotel, but I also knew I had nowhere to be going, had no place that required my return, had no people who were missing me.

An Exclusive King Room would be quite fine, I told the man in the suit. He made an expression of elegant relief, and while escorting me and my only suitcase to the twentieth floor he explained that a wedding party had booked the entire eighth floor and simply could not be separated.

It is entirely our fault, sir, he said with a particular mix of dignity and shame that only a man in such a fine suit can express. *We do wish you a very enjoyable stay at the Grand Claremont Hotel.*

> I felt I was almost speaking to all these people, enduring beside them as all our lives ticked by.

My Exclusive King Room, room 2032, was much like my first love, room 807, only everything was a little larger, every object seemed to have company. The bed, of course, was wider and longer and instead of two sham pillows, there were three and instead of one cylindrical reclining pillow, there were two and instead of four soft down pillows, there were eight and all of them were much larger than their counterparts down in room 807. The chair by the window had a twin and between the two chairs was a low, round table. The ceilings, I realized, were at least two feet higher than in room 807 and the window was thrice as wide. The window, upon closer inspection, was not only a window but also a door, a sliding door that permitted one to pass through it and stand on a narrow balcony.

Over the next few days in room 2032 I began to establish habits quite similar to those of room 807. Did I feel I was betraying my allegiance to room 807 by this new allegiance to room 2032? Indeed I did. But room 807 was getting married and didn't even think of me anymore. I was just trying to carry on. This is reasonable, I told myself, as I moved one of the chairs from the window to the bathroom to the window again, then switched chairs just to be fair, then moved that second chair to the bathroom, back to the window, and switched back to the original chair—well this is just what you do in a room, in whatever room you find yourself within, and after all, I thought, the past is nothing. Once I worked for The Company and that means nothing now. It happens no longer. There is no way to spend any energy on the past. I am just here in this room. Walls. Chairs. Floor. Bed.

I was already beginning to forget room 807, forget what it had meant to me, forget the sensation of being within it. To forget something, to allow myself to forget something, this was somewhat extraordinary behavior for me, as I am afflicted with deeply nostalgic proclivities, constant and pointless yearnings to reach back, always dragging my heels as the clock ticks. To begin to forget something, to even have the thought that the past is nothing—it all felt so radical that I became immediately unrecognizable to myself. I once kept a beer bottle cap for sixteen and a half years because it reminded me of one good launch from a rope swing into a perfect swimming hole on the first good day of a very good summer, a feeling I didn't want to release, a day I didn't want to let slip into the gnaw of forgetting, and now I had become, in an instant, a person who did not care about that bottle cap, about that day, about any feeling I'd ever felt that had faded into the not now.

> The past is nothing, I thought again. It felt cardiovascular. A steep hike.

The past is nothing, I thought again. It felt cardiovascular. A steep hike. I went to sleep having this thought, dreamt of it, woke with it.

Each day, when the maid came, I excused myself to the balcony to give her privacy in her labor. There was no chair on the balcony, and there was barely any standing room, and as I stood there I would sometimes momentarily consider the option I had to lean across the rail far enough that gravity would just end me. But I never did. I somehow identified that as a choice not worth making, which meant I chose to keep living, which meant I chose to keep living in the Grand Claremont Hotel.

One day, when the maid came at her usual hour, I found it was raining rather heavily, so I remained inside room 2032, taking a seat in one of the chairs as she went about her routine. It wasn't until she had almost finished her chores that I realized that I had been intently studying her every movement—the elongation and shortening of her limbs as she vacuumed, the militaristic precision of her bed-making method, her gloved finger searching for dust in the oddest of corners. It seemed the rigor of my attention had implied some sort of unintended message, because just before she left she lingered, looked at me, squinting a little, and said, *Anything else?*

A mix of coyness and fear and determination in her voice. I didn't or maybe couldn't say anything. I must have been breathing heavily because I became critically aware of my lungs in my chest, a sort of pain and pressure in them, as if they were pushing on me from the inside, trying to get out.

She unbuttoned the top button of her shirt and I kept staring at her, still unsure of what it was she was trying to convey to me, or how my staring, a rather nonstandard and perhaps somewhat offensive behavior, had been interpreted to mean something when in fact it meant nothing at all. My inaction apparently gave her the signal to refasten her undone button and flee room 2032 with a cheerful *Goodbye!*

I am not altogether sure how long I lived in room 2032 but at some point a knock came much like the knock that had ended my tenure in room 807. I was certain this would be the end of my stay at the Grand Claremont Hotel, yet I have been very wrong about a great many facts in my life that I was, at one point, certain.

We are deeply sorry to trouble you, the man in the navy suit said. The maid was standing beside him, staring over his shoulder and over my shoulder, into room 2032. *But we have just learned that there will be some construction taking place on the roof of the Hawthorne Building, of which you have an excellent view, but we are afraid the noise and dust will cause too much of a disturbance to your days and nights and we really must insist upon a second relocation.*

I wanted to tell him that I was undisturbed by disturbance, that I no longer hung the *Do Not Disturb* sign on my door, and I also wanted to ask him if he knew why I was still here, and I wanted to say, to confess, really, that though I didn't object to living out all my foreseeable days in the Grand Claremont Hotel, I couldn't understand what had happened that had allowed me to remain here, and though I wanted to know what had transpired that made my tenure in the Grand Claremont Hotel possible, I also wasn't sure I wanted to know or could even stand to know the reasons I was still here. Maybe one shouldn't lift the hood of some machines. I said nothing, waited.

We really must insist, sir, that you allow us to offer you more peaceful accommodations. An Executive Ultra-King Suite on the twenty-ninth floor is available for your occupancy. You needn't even pack up, as we will be happy to take care of that burden for you.

At this the maid entered the room and began packing my meager things as the man in the suit guided me by the shoulder down the hallway to the elevator, up to the twenty-ninth floor, down the hallway, and into the Executive Ultra-King Suite, room 2901, which was not just one but, in fact, four rooms: a sitting room with two sofas and one chair, a dining room with a large table, a bathroom with a tub you could nearly swim a lap in, and a bedroom containing a bed that was roughly the size of the entirety of room 807. Every room had large windows and the ceilings rose to such a height that I felt I was in a cathedral, or one of those opulent old banks built when dollars must have seemed more hopeful than they have turned out to be.

This must be the finest accommodation in the entire hotel, I said.

We are so delighted you approve, sir.

I wanted to ask the man in the suit where he lived, whether he had a room in the hotel, and if he did, what did his room look like, and if he didn't, what did his home look like, and if he had a home and not a room, were there any other people who shared this home with him, and how did it feel to leave his home each morning to come here, to this building full of room-homes, temporary and semitemporary places for people who were on their way somewhere or lost along the way somewhere or people who did not fit into any category at all. But I said nothing to him, just felt a knot tighten in my gut, a knot in my throat, a knot in my head, as if I were a piece of rope meant to demonstrate how it's done—barrel knot, square knot, slipknot, and so on. At some point perhaps I may have known how to tie such things.

Your luggage will be delivered shortly, he said as he backed out the door, leaving me to the Executive Ultra-King Suite. *I don't wish to disturb you any further.*

Alone in the Executive Ultra-King Suite I could hear a slight drone, some sort of noise the suite had created, it seemed, by its own vastness. I walked from room to room, touched the various fabrics and surfaces—marble, stainless steel, linen, slate, hardwood, tile, sheepskin, bearskin, other kinds of skin, soft sheets, downy blankets, pillows, throw pillows, accent pillows, glass.

As the droning increased in volume, I wondered if I had missed some turn at some point in my life and now I was just passing through a series of spaces that had never been meant for me. The drone became even louder, that or my own moroseness was having the best of me. No, I wouldn't let it, I thought. What I needed was a brisk walk, yes, in fact that was all I needed, though I also knew it was possible I may set out for this walk and never return. My skin went damp as this possibility began to seem more possible. The drone became louder. My bowels shifted like cargo on a storm-thrown ship.

I tried to steady myself against a nearby window and either my hand was trembling or the glass was trembling or everything was being shaken by the drone, and I wondered if there might be a wild animal somewhere in this room to which my body had become aware and was reacting biologically before I could react consciously. I looked all over all the rooms and found nothing save for the luxuries of the Executive Ultra-King Suite. The drone had reached such a volume I felt my teeth shaking in their gums.

My bowels shifted like cargo on a storm-thrown ship.

I ran down the hallway and jumped into a waiting elevator, took that elevator to the lobby, but when I arrived in the lobby I was still on floor twenty-nine. I pressed the LOBBY key again. The doors shut and I believe I sensed the elevator move, yet when the doors opened again I was still on floor twenty-nine. I looked for additional instructions on how to operate the elevator but found none. I pressed LOBBY again, harder this time—I meant it. The elevator door shut and I was so sure I felt the elevator descend, that familiar sinking, but when the doors opened a third time I was still on the twenty-ninth floor.

Well, I am not one to allow such absurdity to continue. I won't let myself be made a fool. I went back to 2901, the suite, that very special place. *What is this?* I asked myself, but even my own voice could not be heard over the drone.

What a person should remember at times like these, when all normalcy seems to have left you, is that all things begin and end in the mind. Anything can be in there and anything can be taken out—anything, any single thing, by which I mean everything can be taken out and whatever remains is what you are, not the sensations you feel, the food you eat, not the people you seem to know or the objects you own or the people you seem to own or the objects that have known you all your life. You're not even the memories you can remember or even the thoughts you can think. You are something below all those things. You are the little dog at the bottom of the pile, no not even the dog but the smallest flea on the smallest dog at the bottom of the pile. Even less than that, even less and still somehow more than anything else—that's what you are. And when you can remember this everything becomes very still and you can move around easily, as if lucid in a dream.

I noticed a door I'd overlooked upon my arrival to 2901, and opening it I found a large closet in which my few clothes had been hung. Also there were three navy suits and three white shirts monogrammed with the Grand Claremont Hotel logo. There was also a navy telephone mounted onto the wall of the closet and as I stood there, awash in the drone, breathing the reassuring scent of clean laundry, the phone began to ring, and though I couldn't hear it over the drone a knuckle-sized red light flashed to let me know.

I came up with the closest thing I could manage to specifically want or need or desire—a removal.

As I lifted the phone to my ear the drone ceased, and I spoke that sad question—*Hello?*

Good afternoon, sir, and how are you feeling today?

I stood there with my mouth open.

Is there anything else you need? Anything at all?

I gathered myself to answer—*In fact, yes*—I believe, *perhaps, there is something wrong with the elevator.*

And what, sir, might be wrong with the elevator?

Well, in fact, it seems to be stuck on this floor, won't allow me down to the lobby.

I don't understand, sir—

I got into the elevator here on the twenty-ninth floor intending to go down to the lobby so I might reach the street, and—

Technically—the voice interrupted—*an elevator's job, by its very definition, is to elevate, and here at the Grand Claremont Hotel, our elevators do what they are defined to do.*

Oh, I said, unable to protest such an allegiance to words, *should I take the stairs down instead?*

Sir, I must admit I am confused by your question. Is there anything else that you need?

That I need?

Yes—is there something unavailable to you on the twenty-ninth floor that you are trying to procure?

Well, I just thought I would go out for—

Out?

Out of the building, yes, into the street, so that I could—

Sir, let's not be so hasty. There's no reason to take such drastic actions. We can have anything sent up that you might need or desire.

Well.

Is there anything else that you need or desire, sir?

I may have forgotten what I needed, or perhaps forgotten what a need is, what a desire is, what the difference between these things might be, but eventually I came up with the closest thing I could manage to specifically want or need or desire—a removal.

There's a noise in this room.

A noise, sir?

Yes, a kind of . . . humming. It's hard to describe. It started softly, then became louder and louder, a kind of throbbing, even, though it has stopped now, though I'm sure it's not gone, not really gone. It's really more of a feeling, actually, than a noise—

But the line, I realized, had gone dead. I braced for the drone to reemerge, but all that came was a knock at the door—one knock—barely a knock at all. The man in the suit was there, all intent and smiling.

You've reported a noise, sir.

How did you get up here?

Sir?

Did you take the elevator?

Sir, I am here to attend to this issue of a noise. Would you mind if I stepped into the suite to inspect this issue further?

I stepped aside to let him in.

And will you take the elevator back down to the lobby, is that correct?

But he did not seem to hear my question or perhaps heard and ignored me. I felt distracted by his suit and realized that I too was wearing a suit such as his. The maid came in, hurried past me to join the man in the suit in the sitting room, who was squinting up at each corner, staring into one then another, another. As the maid passed me two strands of hair wafted from her head. One landed on a shaggy white rug in front of me and the other on my left shoe.

For a few minutes, I felt unable to move. I stared down at those two strands of hair, black and thick, and though I realize that technically hair is dead, they each seemed to be breathing, fluttering, moving toward me, telling me something.

The man in the suit and the maid were looking around the room, looking, it seemed, for the drone or whatever had caused the drone. Some time passed in which they looked for the drone and I stared down at these hair strands. At times I would look up to see them examining something, or tapping at the windows, peeking under chair cushions, under rugs. I imagined Company Headquarters going on without me, how my old cot was sleeping its object sleep without me. There were so many people in the world for whom The Company had no use. I shut my eyes. I knew it was not the end.

What I can say is that the view from the Grand Claremont Penthouse is magnificent—I have always been humbled by the ocean. It has always worked easily on me. True, I cannot actually see the ocean from my window in the Grand Claremont Penthouse, for this is a landlocked country and the ocean is perhaps a thousand miles from us. Yet I can feel it in the air. I remember it still.

Now I stand at the window all day, watching my breath gather wet on the glass, fade, gather, and fade again. I do not bother moving the chair anymore. I am only slightly aware of putting food or water into myself. Sometimes I think of room 807, or 2032, or 2901—but more often I find myself fixed on the memory of those two strands of hair and what they told me about living and dying, though we all know there is only one thing to know about living and dying and since it's told all the time, all the time, I won't bother with it now. 🏢

Philip Metres

THE HOUSE AT LONG LAKE

How a house is a self
& else, a seeping into
of light deciding the day.
    A house so close

it breathes as the lake
    breathes. How a lake
is a shelf, an eye,
    a species of seeing,

burbling of tongues
    completing the shore.
How a loon is a probing,
    a genus of dreams,

encyclopedia of summer.
    Unsummable house
by the lake, generous hinge
    opening us. I loved,

in folds of sleep, to hear
        the back door's yawn
& click. You gliding
        down toward shore

& dawn, beyond all frames,
        reconciling yourself to
bracing Long Lake.
        Into its ever-opening, you—

COME AGAIN?

ON JEFFREY TENNYSON'S
Hamburger Heaven

TABITHA BLANKENBILLER

Somewhere in the Buckley, Washington, library you'll find a copy of Jeffrey Tennyson's *Hamburger Heaven: The Illustrated History of the Hamburger* with twenty-five 1996 checkout stamps. I read Tennyson's book for a year, studying each page's playful layout and memorizing his cheeky captions, as rapturous as scripture. His history recounted the sensational White Castle slider revolution, the drive-in neon constellation sky of California, and the coffee-shop-counter sentinels of respite along Route 66. An imagined America is pieced together in Tennyson's pages, an America of families that dress up for dinner with the same ceremony as they do for church, of smiling waitresses in scalloped-lace aprons and starchy paper hats delivering toasted, melting, salty divinity to waiting cars. As he describes this golden age, Tennyson's voice lilts off the page in a cadence that is self-aware (yes, he's talking about hamburgers) but relentlessly reverent (god damn it, he *loves* hamburgers): "At the local drive-in, burger-bearing dreamgirls such as Brenda helped put the *amour* in glamour, and the kitsch in the kitchen." He spoke about his favorite food in a way that didn't simply make me want to listen. It made me want to live in its world.

Through *Hamburger Heaven* I could imagine an adolescent life in which each day started with a freshly pressed poodle skirt and ended at the drive-in. If I could magically slip into Tennyson's collection of original road stop photographs and toothy advertisements, I'd have everything my postmodern teenage life lacked: friends, acceptance, milk shakes.

That year, the year of *Hamburger Heaven*, I was failing to fit in to my new school in Buckley, a logging town on Mount Rainier's plateau. We'd moved from the big city district of Tacoma, with its hundred combinations of languages, faiths, interests, abilities. Tacoma was a population of contours and shades. Buckley was as diversely flat as the open glen where Bambi's mom was mowed down.

Social acceptance was governed by a clique of preened, identical Abercrombie girls who'd known each other since birth, who tracked together into adolescence. Girls who still, as I stumble across them in my Facebook periphery, attend each other's birthdays and LuLaRoe parties as the next generation of cheerleaders and quarterbacks toddle at their knees.

I wore T-shirts screened with puns, not sexy brands. I turned in writing assignments with extra pages. I had bad skin.

I knew I was unacceptable there as myself, but I didn't know what else to be. In a stunning feat of naïveté I held on to the Disney afternoon special notion that if you keep shining as Your Best Self, others will come around.

So when we were asked to present a demonstrative, teachable process to our classmates, I reached for the book I wouldn't let the library take back, which ends with Tennyson's perfect hamburger recipe.

"We need to go to a butcher," I told my mom.

"Can't I pick you up a pound of hamburger from Fred Meyer?" she pleaded, having already suffered my nerdy requests for calligraphy pens, road trip stops at Oregon Trail landmarks, and out-of-print George Washington biographies.

We negotiated for grocery store ground beef purchased the same day. I borrowed Mom's electric skillet and set up my tiny kitchen next to the overhead projector. "It's important not to overhandle the meat," I said as I formed the patty, walking straight into a joke I didn't understand and tipping the girls into a fit of barely veiled laughter. The half pound sizzled, and my teacher opened a window. I flipped it only once, just as Tennyson decreed, resisting the urge to oppress the swelling beef mass with a spatula smoosh.

"And that," I said, raising my sandwich to the popcorn-ceiling sky, "is a perfect hamburger."

I took the paper plate, the first dish I'd ever cooked by myself, back to my desk. As a presentation on proper Tamagotchi maintenance set up, I took a bite I can still remember. The textural harmony of butter-toasted bun and a blushing pink middle, warm and rich with a divine balance of salt and grease.

"I bet you she eats the whole thing," I heard one of the girls fake whisper two seats behind me.

"What a fatty."

Without speaking I stood from my desk, holding the plate, and walked my shame to the garbage can.

That weekend, I didn't bring *Hamburger Heaven* to the checkout desk. I let it drop into the mawing black hole of the book return and retreated deeper into myself.

In the next two decades the memories of the book would flit in and out of my mind—when I had my first White Castle slider on the Las Vegas Strip, or whenever I saw a guy in a TV commercial mash his innocent burgers into the grill grates. When I began working on my first book, a collection of essays about food and the creative process, I couldn't get Tennyson's joy and design out of my head. *I should tell him*, I thought, and went to look up his contact info.

The top Google result for Jeffrey Tennyson, Author? A *New York Times* obituary.

Tennyson died in 2006, thirteen years after his omnivore's opus was published. He was fifty-four years old, and lost his life to HIV complications.

I opened a new window and purchased the book I'd only leased in grade school. It arrived forty-eight hours later, hours I spent thinking of all that Tennyson had missed. The resurgence of quality over the commodity burgers of his final days: the national expansions of Shake Shack and Five Guys and In-N-Out. I wanted to read all the biting captions he'd have written for the Heart Attack Grill and Guy Fieri ("this flame-broiled vaudevillian's schtick is rarely well done"). Pop culture was poised for a burger-worshipping renaissance, and he was cruelly, needlessly robbed of the chance to play maestro.

I spent a full afternoon with my sixth-grade best friend, revisiting the escape that Tennyson erected from his collection of neon photography and discarded menus. I marveled anew at the crisp, immaculate lines of the art deco White Tower restaurants that have vanished from their Midwest street corners. I grinned at his turns of phrase ("at Ships, the out-of-this-world, Ship-Shape Burger sold better than the hotcakes").

At the back of the book I found my favorite section: a peek into Tennyson's personal collection of hamburger art and memorabilia. When I flipped to my favorite painting, an eighties psychedelic burger in midflight, I noticed a rendering that my younger self hadn't registered: a New York burger stop with a rainbow aesthetic that clashes with its menacing, darkened doorway. To the right, stairs descend into the subway underground, where we catch a man in motion, clad head to toe in black. He is more shadow than flesh; his head sags in resignation, in hurry, an entreaty for escape.

The caption: *Painting by the author*.

I knew that posture, that willing of self away from whispers and glare. That wish to disappear into a time when you belonged. Just as I knew its companion fear—that such a place doesn't exist.

There was never a Hamburger Heaven. There were instead the same small, shitty towns and smaller-minded people, in all eras and all stages of the drive-in's life-span. Tennyson and I could only offer up our overtipping hearts in the world we had, and hope that raw, unrepentant ardor was a beacon to another. Just as Tennyson's had been to me.

Hamburger Heaven nested an imperceptible idea into my twelve-year-old mind: The things you love, the obsessions you can read about all hours of the day and recount so blissfully your words come out in song, the passions that make you stand out with zero chill—that affection will not always be a liability. One day it will become your greatest asset. What people remember you for, even after your departure.

I needed that revelation, even if it took me twenty years and two dozen checkouts to grasp it. Maybe Jeffrey Tennyson did, too.

ON JOHN HAMPSON'S

Saturday Night at the Greyhound

JON MICHAUD

Recently I was browsing through lists of circadian novels: novels that take place in a single day. I'm in the middle of writing one, so it seemed like a useful way to avoid work. Amid the usual suspects—*Ulysses, Mrs. Dalloway, Under the Volcano,* and *One Day in the Life of Ivan Denisovich*—I came across *Saturday Night at the Greyhound* by John Hampson, a book I'd never heard of. The listicle's blurb said that the novel related the events of a single dramatic night in a Derbyshire pub. I ordered a copy right away.

While I waited for the book to arrive from the UK, I procrastinated further by reading up on the author. Born in 1901, Hampson descended from a once-prosperous family that, according to the writer Christopher Hawtree, made its name in the Midlands through the theater and the brewing industry. The collapse of the family business early in Hampson's childhood meant that he grew up in poverty. A sickly child, he was educated at home. He labored at a variety of jobs (munitions worker, billiard marker, waiter, chef) and, desperate for income, even resorted to stealing and reselling books (in particular, copies of *Gray's Anatomy*), for which he did time in Wormwood Scrubs prison. Hampson finally found steady employment in 1925 as a nurse and companion to a child with Down syndrome. Reliable work allowed him to write fiction.

Saturday Night at the Greyhound was Hampson's first published novel. Leonard Woolf at the Hogarth Press, who had turned down an earlier novel (*Go Seek a Stranger*) from Hampson because of its candid depiction of homosexual life, took the book on. The debut was an instant success, reprinted three times in its first week of release. Since its publication in 1931, the book's admirers have included Graham Greene and E. M. Forster, and there is good reason for their admiration. In its narrative efficiency, *Saturday Night at the Greyhound*, which is only 150 pages long, calls to mind such distilled masterpieces as *Chronicle of a Death Foretold* and *The Death of Ivan Ilyich*. Like those books it also captures a particular cultural and historical moment, in this case Britain between the wars. By compressing his characters' lifetimes of futility and social stasis into a handful of hours, the author creates an incendiary milieu that is primed to explode.

Hampson originally conceived of the novel as a play, and it retains a three-act structure as well as the dramatic unities of time, action, and place. Written in a direct, unadorned style, it opens with an overture introducing the scheming, self-serving Mrs. Tapin, an elderly resident of the hamlet of Grovelace who works as a charwoman at the eponymous local pub: "She had seen fourteen men take over the Greyhound in her time. Fourteen and none of them had made it pay." Mrs. Tapin herself is one of the obstacles to making the pub financially viable; she steals from her employers with brazen self-entitlement. It takes fewer than ten pages for Hampson to establish her character, set the scene, and foreshadow the dramatic events to come. "The village did not make strangers welcome," she observes. "Those who went wrong were wise to stay away."

Mrs. Tapin has a daughter, Clara, conceived out of wedlock with the local Squire Grovedon. Young and pretty, Clara tends bar at the Greyhound and fools around with its proprietor, Fred Flack, a charismatic "drunkard" and "liar" who is running the pub into the ground. Fred, in Mrs. Tapin's exacting opinion, is "slipshod and easy to cheat."

While Fred drinks, glad-hands, and plays cards with his customers, his wife, Ivy, and her young brother, Tom Oakley, do the actual work of the pub's operation. The otherwise-sensible Tom is besotted with his sister in a way that verges on the incestuous. He believes that they could make the Greyhound successful if only she would leave Fred and fire the Tapin women. Ivy is well aware of Fred's serial infidelities but refuses to cast him aside. For her part, Clara sees her affair with Fred as a possible way out of Grovelace. Fred, meanwhile, has been keeping secret the severity of the Greyhound's financial distress as he considers running off with Clara. Like a bomb maker rolling out a fuse, Hampson expertly unfolds the poisonous and dysfunctional dynamic among these five in the book's first part.

That fuse takes flame in the novel's second section. Hampson introduces two outsiders to this knot of proletarian deceit and grievance: Roy Grovedon, the (legitimate) son of the squire, and Ruth Dorme, a wealthy single woman from London whom Roy hopes to marry. Boredom has driven Ruth from the capital for the weekend. Intrigued by the provincials she sees while dining at the Greyhound, she decides to stay the night to study them further: "These people, she felt, really lived; compared to them, she was a dilettante." Roy, having grown up nearby, in the squire's hall, has little time for Ruth's amateur anthropology. He goes home to his father's house. Ruth would be an easy character to satirize but Hampson, to his credit, manages the more difficult task of fleshing her out while never letting her off the hook for her condescension.

The book's final section delivers the explosive climax and revelations we've been expecting, along with a gruesome surprise: a scene of shocking animal cruelty that made me clench my teeth as I read. Hampson offers his characters few morsels of redemption or hope. To do otherwise would feel like a betrayal of this minutely observed chronicle of working-class paralysis. Only Ruth, the monied interloper, who operates as a stand-in for the reader, escapes. As she leaves the pub, she thinks, "The world was large and she had stumbled accidentally on a patch of human misery. . . . Nothing one said, did, or thought made the slightest difference."

The way out for Hampson was to turn misery into art: He was an important force in the Birmingham Group, a loose collective of writers and artists who met regularly in a Birmingham pub. Dedicated to the realistic portrayal of working-class life, Hampson and other members, including Leslie Halward, Walter Allen, Peter Chamberlain, and Ivan Roe, cultivated younger writers. For example, Hampson helped Walter Brierley place his debut novel, *Means-Test Man*, about an unemployed Derbyshire miner, with Methuen. Hampson published a second book with Hogarth (*O Providence*) and later novels with Heinemann, but never produced another work of the quality of *Saturday Night at the Greyhound*. Succinct in structure and potent in effect, it deserves its place among the great circadian novels.

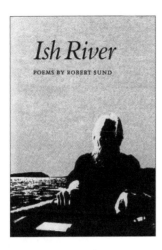

ON ROBERT SUND'S
Ish River

JOSHUA JAMES AMBERSON

I read Robert Sund's slim *Ish River* because I hated large collected works of poetry. I was a twenty-two-year-old aspiring poet with a lot of half-formed ideas about what poetry was, or should be, and I had recently begun working at the largest independent bookstore in Olympia, Washington. On my shifts, I would often linger in the store's ample poetry section, shyly striking up conversations with the customers who frequented the aisle as I shelved books and made displays. Every time I came across a book with "Collected Poems" in the title my face scrunched the way a cat's does when it smells another cat's pee—nose turned up, tongue slightly protruding—because I believed these books were an injustice. Poetry was written to be read in short, intentional bursts—not these long, disjointed marathons through an author's body of work.

Sund's collected works had just been released and all of the older poets from around town were stopping into the bookstore to pick it up, telling me how important Sund had been, how I should drop everything and read it. And the thing was: I wanted to. Sund, I learned in this small flurry of excitement, had at one time been one of Washington State's most recognized poets. But as his books had gone out of print, his work had fallen between the cracks. I also learned how he had lived like a hermit in tiny shacks, doing calligraphy, translating Swedish poetry, perpetually broke. This was exactly the kind of artist I wanted to read. But I was stubborn and even though I'd never mentioned my hatred of all collected poems to anyone, I felt I had to stick by my beliefs—even my unvoiced, inner ones.

Luckily, not too long after, a copy of *Ish River* came across the buying table. Overshadowed by his more cohesive and formally innovative 1969 debut, *Bunch Grass*, *Ish River* is a brief, pieced-together assortment of poems, written over the course of fifteen years. It came out in 1983 from San Francisco's North Point Press. I took it home that afternoon and, sitting on my porch, opened to the short poem that serves as the book's preface:

> "Ish River"—
>   like breath,
>   like mist rising from a hillside.
> Duwamish, Snohomish,
>   Stillaguamish, Samish,
> Skokomish, Skykomish. . . all
>   the ish rivers.

I was stunned. I had grown up in the rural outskirts of Snohomish, Washington, and, still carrying the narrow view of my teen years, considered it a place devoid of art and culture. But here it was, alongside all these other familiar names of my home state, as poetry. The book's nondescript white cover with light gray text—the words almost disappearing into their canvas—was the same color scheme I saw when I looked up from its pages. More than anything else I'd read, this was a book about where I came from.

In *Ish River*, Sund travels western Washington, dropping into towns whose names I'd never seen in a work of literature before—Chehalis, Issaquah, Elma. I laughed out loud when Sund finds himself in Everett, the largest city in Snohomish County, where I had lived just a few years prior: "Taking a walk in the early morning / in Everett. Not the most / beautiful place in the world." The poem distilled the particular sadness of a city I had known my entire life. It's a place where "sad architects are on the loose everywhere." A place that "is a stranded ship, a museum." Where "there are hardly any flowers."

While other poets focus solely on the Northwest's natural wonder, Sund manages to casually combine that beauty with its forgotten, discarded side. In the poem "Mean Dog on Country Road," he writes:

> Walking down from Harris's
> place on Grand Ridge
> singing aloud to trees on both
> sides of me,

> I pass an ugly pink house
> set in a little hollow below the road.
> A police dog begins to bark, then
> comes running through the junk-
> strewn yard
> and stops at the edge of the road . . .

Flanked by trees, passing trashed front lawns? This was the rural landscape I knew. Maybe for the first time, I saw that my childhood home's driveway of broken-down cars was a poem, the pile where we burned our trash was a poem, the blue-tarp-covered lawn mower parts we hid in the woods were a poem. I grew up on "strange roads / that lead back to the city" and this was something to write about and embrace, not something to pretend never happened.

As I read *Ish River*, I tried to loosen my associations and imagine what it would be like to experience the book as an outsider, and I felt that the poems were still interesting.

In many ways this is what was so exciting to me about the book: the idea that I could write about home and have it translate beyond the area, beyond associations. The idea that names could become poems in their own right, that the "Snohomish, Stillaguamish, Samish, Skokomish, Skykomish" litany could reverberate in the head of any reader. And even though Sund doesn't directly address the meanings of these names, *Ish River* also made me think about how they don't just represent rivers but entire tribes of people. Something about seeing the names together, in a place and form I didn't expect them to be, made me realize that I'd grown up surrounded by these names but knew next to nothing about their history.

In the Coast Salish family of languages of which these tribes are a part, "ish" can be translated a variety of ways. It's been interpreted as "water" or "river" (which would make Sund's title a bit repetitive) but "people of" or "land of" are also common. This is how I've most often heard "Snohomish" translated: "lowland people" or "land of the low people." The fact that each of the tribes Sund lists long ago chose to share their name with the river they lived on suggests that they considered themselves inseparable from the river— the river was part of their identity, the river was life. In time, the "Snohomish, Stillaguamish, Samish, Skokomish, Skykomish" litany came to mean something more to me: it was a reminder of whom the land belonged to, a new perspective on the place I called home.

The simple, meditative poems in *Ish River* don't move me the way they did when I first read them thirteen years ago. But I'll forever be in debt to the book for helping me see place as essential to identity. It showed me how the personal specifics of place, when put to the page, can become universal, and how the place you're from always holds more layers to uncover—histories that can complicate your understanding and histories that weren't recorded, histories you can never know.

ON HERMAN LeROY EMMET'S

Fruit Tramps

CHESTON KNAPP

They were days of uncertainty and shame, desperation and anger, those many long months in the midaughts when I couldn't find a job, when the only part of my world that didn't seem to be shrinking was my credit card debt. A buddy and I had recently packed everything we owned into our cars and driven across the country, from Virginia to Oregon—the night before we left someone broke into my car and stole a large tub of my clothes. In the place we'd rented sight unseen, a squalid 2BR with fungal wall-to-wall carpet and faux-wood paneling, thoughts of money, of how to solve for its lack, tyrannized my days. It hasn't dimmed over the intervening decade-plus, the memory of the claustrophobia that dogged me then, the persistent feeling of *Fuck. Me.* What help my family could offer was meager and, therefore, taxed usuriously by guilt, so I told myself I'd do *anything*, and polished off job applications the way some folks do Sudoku. To sell Xerox machines and insurance policies and ecologically friendly outerwear. To be a financial planner and busboy and intern. I applied for so many jobs that I lost count and track, and so was baffled when I received a message offering me work at an outfit called "Wine by Joe." At some point, I guess, I'd applied to work at a winery.

It was early fall and the man, not Joe, said he could use some hands for the harvest. I'd been working from before I was legally able to, and yet never had I had the wand of synecdoche flourished in my direction, never had I been transmogrified into a "hand"—it diminished me but good. And the work was hard and the hours were long, is how Hemingway would've phrased it. The day started at 7:00 AM—I had to leave our place no later than 6:00 to make it to the warehouse in Dundee on time—and I could expect to work until at least 7:00 PM, though routinely later. My most common assignment upon arriving was to stand along a conveyor belt with one or two other hands and remove pieces of stems and berries gone busted or moldy or both and earwigs and stinkbugs from the otherwise good globular clusters of fruit. Sometimes we were told that certain vats of grapes were special, that they'd become a rarefied type of wine we'd never be able to afford, FancyAss Millionaire wine. And into those vats, feeling smug and knackered mad, I'd let fall an extra helping of rotted fruit and earwigs, imagining a

trophy wife of the future musing, "What's that I taste on the finish? Smooshed stinkbug?" When I returned home at night I didn't have the energy or time to do anything but sleep.

While relieved, and proud, to be working, I started to recognize, during one of my seemingly endless shifts, the sick joke that was afoot, ye olde capitalistic rope-a-dope, that the claustrophobia of the unemployed isn't much different from the claustrophobia of the overworked and underpaid. To work so hard and yet still not feel like you're gaining ground or, worse, to feel like you might even still be losing it is a situation masterfully portrayed in *Fruit Tramps*, Herman LeRoy Emmet's tender and gripping portrait of the Tindals, a family of white migrant workers. "We have busted our ass for years, but it just don't pay," says the Tindal matriarch, Linda. "We're pickers. We always have been pickers. It's in the blood. My mamma and daddy done it. L. H.'s folks's done it. All our kin done it. We've tried to get away from it, but there ain't much else we can do."

Over seven years spanning the late seventies and early eighties, Emmet spent chunks of time living and working with L. H. (Luther Henry) and Linda Tindal and their two kids, taking the notes and photographs that would become *Fruit Tramps*. The book owes an obvious debt to the seminal documentary project of James Agee and Walker Evans, *Let Us Now Praise Famous Men*, but Emmet's sensibility, aided considerably by the Tindals' staggering generosity, is distinct enough that the work stands on its own.

The text that makes up the book's first half consists of anecdotes, unscripted interviews, and short domestic scenes—casual sketches pulled from the fabric of the Tindals' days. They're written with unornamented prose and feel like snapshots, which lends to the structure the lyrical, mosaic quality of a family album. Emmet doesn't exalt or romanticize the Tindals' suffering, but neither does he ignore it. Describing L. H. early on, Emmet writes, "In the dim light, you could barely see that his left foot had four toes; the small one had been blown off by gunshot. He was missing half his right heel; a bullet had gone through that and had left a hole that just about passed daylight." And a section called, simply, "Stumps," begins: "Luther Henry got all his teeth pulled today. Linda lost five with four left. L. H. lost fifteen with none left. He's thirty-five. She's twenty-three." But not all the sections are so brutal. The best reveal and revel in the joy and intimacy of a strong family fighting against the odds, like when the brakes on L. H.'s truck go out and he heroically fixes them by pouring a beer into the master brake cylinder, joking after, "Bet you never learned that in college."

It's unavoidable, though—the realization that the game is so totally and obviously rigged against the Tindals begins to inflect the written sections with that terrifying suspicion that the walls are closing in on you. Emmet's remarkable accomplishment with this book is one of pacing. Right when you start thinking you can't read any longer, he switches tack, turning to photos to tell the story. And Emmet truly shines as a photographer.

The photos, understated black-and-white shots in the classic documentary mode, make full use of the access the Tindals granted and overflow with the particulars of their work and lives. The first in the series shows L. H. climbing an apple tree in South Carolina, framed by tree leaves, and there's a cart below and his eyes are rolled up in his head and he looks maybe a touch possessed and yet echoing in your head are his words from the preceding pages, "All I want is a little respect for me and my family, so we can live in dignity." L. H.'s forceful candor humbled me—my memories of privation, sharp but brief, have been found to be, as it were, wanting—and even with many thousands more words I still couldn't do justice to the way this project makes you want to give him, them, that dignity and more.

In addition to stinkwigging, I had one other primary responsibility at the winery—punch downs. After the grapes had been juiced, they sat in a giant bin, the skins floating on top of what, with time, would become wine. These skins would harden into a ruddy concrete and, in order to ensure the wine got the most out of the skins, I had to take a giant plunger and force them back under the juice. This feels like a metaphor for what the book achieves, putting us in touch as it does with the people who, in a way, feed us. And so I'll leave off with a quote from L. H., to whom Emmet so deftly gives voice: "I fruit tramp to survive that's what I do. I like the freedom. I choose the life. *Fruit tramp* says what I am. *Migrant* don't. That's what someone else says I am."

"Dramatic, superbly ironic . . . A narrative that seduces with style. Her best writing." —*The New Statesman*

kathy acker

ON KATHY ACKER'S
In Memoriam to Identity

RUBY BRUNTON

I knew Kathy Acker's infamous blonde crop, her upper arm and back tattoos, her androgynous layers of clothing and heavy metal jewelry long before I was familiar with her writing. I had seen her quotes, passages, book covers, and photos shared by fans across Tumblr, Instagram, and Twitter many times; I had researched a little into her backstory; I knew many of her confidantes and collaborators by name or through friends. I knew I was attracted to her, that if I read her writing I would find something essential to me in it—but I held back. She terrified me a little, as if she would lead me down some rabbit hole I'd never be able to get out of. Acker remained but a fantasy in my mind, a writer who would become one of my greatest influences if I'd just read her work. Finally I allowed myself to dip into her earlier works, such as the Kathy novels and *Blood and Guts in High School*. However, her early works, while still challenging, tend to be easier to follow, more narrative, descriptive, and better received by critics.

Acker's identity as a writer has always been about both her image and her texts. This two-pronged-ness was polarizing in her lifetime, and still is. The mythologizing of certain writers horrifies purists and represents something unpopular in many literary circles, where it is often felt that the work should speak for itself. And yet the peroxide hairdo, Vivienne Westwood corsets, motorcycles, and black-and-white photos that adorn many of her book covers are as much a part of who she is as the writing. They are certainly so much of what called me to her, beckoning like the bad-boy narcissistic alcoholics I am unfortunately attracted to. Perhaps this was where the fear began, the knowledge that if I got too close to Acker I'd fall for her and then have my heart broken. Perhaps I saw myself in her characters more than I liked.

Acker's 1990 novel, *In Memoriam to Identity*, appealed to me for its title and invocation of Arthur Rimbaud, a favorite poet and another mythic literary figure. The lure of the tragic romantic poet to the punk writer of a century later is clear: Rimbaud defied authority and lived as a libertine but ached with the pain of forbidden love. The title fits our present age, when "identity" has become a dominant thread in public discourse—and yet at the time of the book's release, feels also like a farewell; the book arrived in the world when Acker had reached the end of her brief fame, as outlined in Chris Kraus's seminal biography, *After Kathy Acker*. The year before *In Memoriam*'s publication, Acker fled London soon after receiving accusations of plagiarism. The book was mostly written while she was hiding out from the press's attacks in Paris. "One of the ways of making your work legitimate is to work it through yourself," Sylvère Lotringer, quoted in Kraus's biography, says of Acker's autofiction. The plagiarism incident, along with other events from Acker's life, makes its way into the narrative as Acker splits and hides parts of herself in her text. To some critics, this felt like burying what was most alive and compelling about Acker's work—that is to say, Acker herself. "The characters in Kathy Acker's nine novels are far less intriguing than the characters on [the cover of] some of them," wrote Stephen Schiff in the *New York Times*. This feels to me like a misunderstanding. Why can't Acker be all of them?

In Memoriam to Identity tracks three disparate but not entirely unrelated protagonists, horcruxes of the author. Rimbaud endures childhood abuses and the torment of falling in love with a married man. Capitol, a promiscuous performance artist, avoids being pimped out by her sleazy money-hungry brother, also called Rimbaud, by running away to New York. (This move resembles Acker's own flight from London back to New York following her forced public apology for the perceived plagiarism of Harold Robbins, a writer who later stated he didn't even care if she had.) Airplane, a young woman, suffering a nightmarish Stockholm syndrome and tethered to her rapist, finds work in the dingiest of sex clubs, a venue facetiously named Fun City.

The constant abuse of these three characters, along with the spliced, nonchronological narrative that places Rimbaud in Nazi-occupied France—the real Rimbaud died half a century earlier—makes for uncomfortable reading. Acker's insistence that her two heroines are "girls who like to fuck" feels at odds with the descriptions of the sex, which rarely reads as enjoyable. This led me to question the use of the verb "like": does feeling the need to fuck often necessarily mean the characters like doing it, or is what they "like" the escape? Reading Acker's work in the throes of a toxic and consuming obsession of my own, then reading the book again having escaped, I could see the "like" morph in both directions.

Acker was committed to the idea that the sexual act could lead to profound self-discovery, to a theoretical metaphysical sphere that was otherwise inaccessible. Airplane, mirroring Acker, flings herself into a tempestuous affair with a married German reporter. Their sadistic sexual encounters leave her in physical and psychological pain. The affair resembles how most of Acker's relationships are described: intense, sexually and sometimes physically violent, short-lived, and fast-forgotten. "Acker would pursue BDSM in her writing and life to a point where sexuality became . . . the path toward a unified being through violence. . . . sexuality became the means of both finding and losing oneself," writes Kraus. Acker appears fully aware of the danger of pursuing such psychologically unhealthy situations. "Men torture women," Acker decries, and then later in the book, hands Airplane, who endures the suffering of being in love with a sadist, the contradiction many women who love men can understand: "She was now in love with all things that are male. Not hating men, not yet, maybe not ever." Even her portrayal of the genitals themselves betrays Acker's ambivalence about gender. Lines such as "She was sick between her legs where identity *partly* lies" [emphasis mine] and "It's not that I wanted a penis" hint at discomfort with the identity category of "woman" or—worse—"feminist" that the media insisted on foisting upon her and her writing.

In Memoriam to Identity was particularly badly received when it was released. "More postmodern blather from the queen of punk fiction" began her *Kirkus* review. "Acker's linguistic experiments smother [her characters] before they can draw breath," wrote Schiff. Reading Acker's work now is an exercise in understanding. *In Memoriam's*

tragic protagonists are not wholly to blame for the pain they endure; the effects of psychological conditioning and human desire wreak havoc with the notion of free will in romantic choices as they do in much of Acker's work. The reader is made aware of the maps of abuse passed down from caregivers or adult strangers to children, who, in turn, confront personal decisions affected by their turbulent histories. It can make for frustrating reading to encounter characters who time and again return to their abusers without logical explanation, unless readers are able to find radical empathy within themselves.

To stick with the novel and Acker's writing in general necessitates trust, a level of security in the knowledge that you won't know where you're going, and neither does Acker. That doesn't make her a bad guide, rather one who may get you lost, but every time in a new and rewarding location. Maybe, twenty years after her death, we are more ready to hear what she was trying to tell us. Loving Acker's work requires the same empathy and self-assuredness that loving her requires. You can love both only if you are able to accept that she wasn't always sure where she was going, and forgive her for it. 🛡

JOKE

In what I think is a dream,
I look at some manifestation of the past

& say, *I know you're not real.* Someone has to.
As most dream-things do, the past

shapeshifts, reconstitutes itself with new
eyes & a new haircut—the past

made over—& then I forget its name.
I forget what I'm doing with the past.

What is that joke about the river?
It's not really a joke, no more than the past

is really past—the one about water never
being the same water. As it flows past,

the river's current—now *that's* a joke—
is always flowing now, now, now. Past

seven, when I wake from what I think
is a dream—a dream where I tell the past

the truth about itself—it is the present
as it always is. There is no past.

IF I COULD SET THIS TO MUSIC

with heys & handclaps, with yodels
& banjo & what's the chord

that sounds like what the sun does
to leaves late in the day?

If I could find a melody
you could hum along to, then

handclap, handclap, hey!—
& a banjo part that breaks your heart

the way "Rainbow Connection"
always has, admit it, then what?

Harmonica? Oohs & cowbell?
If I could come up

with a chorus, a bridge,
a harmony & a little slide guitar

rising like a question
you didn't know you needed

answered, I think you would
hear me. I think the music

would slip my words inside
the slats of your ribs—

then handclap, hey!
& sleigh bells & a banjo solo

& there goes the sun again,
strumming & plucking the leaves—

Canon

Joan first met Roberto at a coffee shop by campus, where he worked behind the bar. He called her "lady," which wasn't anything special. He called all the female patrons "lady," Joan noticed. One day she sat down and ordered wine and read from Ernest Hemingway's collected stories, marking passages that felt important or profound in mechanical pencil. Joan was a writer, or at least hoped to be. She'd been trying to write a coming-of-age novel for three years, on and off, only making any significant progress when she took copious amounts of amphetamines, which had led to a handful of mental breakdowns. Joan knew she didn't really *enjoy* writing; she was trying to fill some deep void, the origins of which she chose not to explore.

Ashley Whitaker

"What's up, lady? What are you reading? I love that book," Roberto said. He was wiping an empty glass with a towel.

"You've read it?"

"Yeah. The second story is the best one in there. I love the part where the guy bleeds to death after getting impaled by that fake bull."

"I love that part too," Joan said, and it was true, from what she could remember of the scene. She never remembered much of what she read, probably because she was usually high, but she did recall that particular image, of the man in Spain dying in a pool of his own blood.

She watched Roberto as he made a latte. He was wearing the same jeans he always wore, and a pearl-snap cowboy shirt that was at least a size too small and barely grazed his beltline. Joan wondered if it was meant to be a woman's shirt. She took a large gulp of bitter wine, hoping her heart would begin to beat more slowly. She'd overdone her Adderall that day, as she always did, and was all out of weed and opiates, which was what she used to calm herself down and relax. Halfway into her first glass of wine, she ordered another. When Roberto finished with the other customers they continued to talk about books, and it turned out that Roberto had read just about every book ever written. There was nothing Joan had read that he hadn't, and she began to feel inadequate. He told her he was a fiction writer, and she told him she was too. They exchanged email addresses that night, and began sending each other stories. Joan didn't have the emotional capacity to care about Roberto's work, or the attention span to read any of it in its entirety, but he read hers closely, and always gave her positive, encouraging feedback. He made Joan feel good about herself, in a way that she missed. Ever since graduating from college earlier that year, she had lacked an authoritative man to tell her she had talent, to make her feel that her life was worth living, her dreams worth pursuing.

Joan started drinking wine at the coffee shop several times a week, often driving straight over from the Texas capitol, where she was a legislative intern for one of the most conservative members of the statehouse. Although the job was unpaid, only requiring Joan to show up three days a week, for a few hours each day, it kept her afloat by appeasing her divorced parents, who continued to split her astronomical downtown rent fifty-fifty.

Joan brought a different book to read each time she went to the coffee shop, in order to show Roberto how sophisticated her taste was. One day, she was reading Flannery O'Connor's *Everything That Rises Must Converge*.

"Ugh. Flannery O'Connor. She's the worst," Roberto said.

Joan was beginning to notice a pattern with him. While he'd read every book she brought in, the authors fell into only two categories: either they were "the best," or they were "the worst." There was no gray area with Roberto. Joan envied his conviction. She never knew what to feel about any book she read.

"How can you say that about O'Connor? She's canonical," Joan said, placing the book facedown on the bar, embarrassed now at having chosen it.

"There is no *canon*," Roberto said in his heavy Tex-Mex accent, shaking his head, as if he were explaining a painful truth to a child. "Don't believe that bullshit, lady."

One night, after Roberto's shift, he and Joan got high in the alley behind the coffee shop and went to a party together at one of his friend's houses. Standing next to Roberto in the backyard, beneath unseasonal Christmas lights, Joan drank a tallboy of PBR. She felt herself becoming tipsy.

> She'd overdone her Adderall that day, as she always did, and was all out of weed and opiates.

"You're such a unique *person*," she said, swaying toward Roberto. "You're probably the most well-read Mexican I've ever met."

"Yeah? You're probably the most well-read Republican I've ever met," Roberto said. "By far."

"I'm sorry." Joan blushed. "Was that racist?"

"Everything is racist," Roberto said.

"You need to milk that shit. Sprinkle some Spanish phrases in your stories, like Junot Díaz. Academics love it."

Roberto smiled, all knowingly, and said, "Fuck Junot Díaz. He don't know shit, lady."

"Have you ever thought of getting an MFA?" Joan asked. "I'm thinking of applying. I need deadlines to function. I feel like I'm spinning out of orbit."

"No," he said somberly. "Fuck that bullshit."

"Why?"

"I can't," he said. "I never went to college and I need to update my resident alien card. But even if I could, I wouldn't get no fucking MFA."

"I'm sure they would let you in, though. Academics love diversity," said Joan, and then, backtracking, "I don't mean that's the *only* reason they'd let you in. I'm just saying."

"It's okay, lady," he said. "I know what I am."

Growing up, Joan had longed above all things to be Mexican. Her hometown was only half white, and she'd never felt comfortable in her skin. She imagined the popular chola girls at her middle school, with their powdery faces and crispy curls, posing in front of jewel-toned, airbrushed backdrops at the local mall on weekends, carrying the photos around in their purses, to prove they had friends. They coupled up early, many of them getting pregnant at fourteen, thirteen; one girl left the sixth grade at twelve to have a baby. Joan had been so jealous of that girl. All the attention she must have gotten, all the love. On weekends, she'd watch with envy as her Mexican peers walked around the mall slowly, the boy behind the girl, arms wrapped around her waist, simultaneously waltzing and spooning. Joan was always alone back then. Pudgy around the middle with pointy, budding breasts—a body like a fat boy's, she thought, whenever she looked in the mirror. Who would ever want to spoon-waltz with her? She did what she could to fit in. She wore oversized polo shirts over tight, dark-wash jeans, Adidas Superstars, heavy pale makeup, penciled-in eyebrows; she drew a brown line around her lips, put large silver hoops in her ears. Only when Joan left Lewisville did she realize how silly it all was, putting all that effort into appearing marginalized.

> Growing up, Joan had longed above all things to be Mexican.

Joan took a long sip of beer and looked around at the people at the house party, at all of Roberto's friends. They were a bunch of misfits, like him. Some were pale, some were fat, most were white, all of them were unattractive in their own way, but they possessed a collective beauty, Joan thought. She was getting good and drunk, and life was beginning again to seem profound. She watched the bonfire, where his friends were gathered around, smoking cigarettes. Punk rock played quietly on a boom box.

Roberto held out his hand to compare its size with hers. They looked at her small pale hand, doll-like against his big palm. This is something he did often over the next couple of months, because he liked how different their hands were. The comparison made him feel manly, she supposed, and it made her feel petite and fragile.

From the party they went back to his place in Joan's BMW. He lived in a shabby house on East MLK, a part of Austin occupied only by artists and poor people. Joan sat in an old wooden chair in his living room, next to a white plastic table where a vintage baby-blue typewriter sat.

"This is where you write? On that thing?"

"Yes," he said. "This is my baby."

"You fucking hipster," Joan said. And he laughed, a wild, sharp laugh. He packed a bowl and sat across from her, on the other side of the tiny room. There were paintings everywhere, all amateur and shitty and colorful, clearly local artists, she thought. Unless Roberto had painted them himself. Joan didn't ask. Not because she didn't care, but because she was too drunk and high to focus on any one thing for too long, and had already turned her attention to the sad white Labrador who sat pouting in the corner, a bandana around its neck. His name was Norman Mailer, said Roberto.

Then they were talking about the creative writing professor Joan had worked with her last semester in school, Carlos. He was from Del Rio, and had written a collection of short stories called *Del Río*. He had just released a novel called *The Lone Vaquero*.

"That guy sucks. Fuck that guy," Roberto said, taking a hit. He told Joan he'd tried to go to Carlos's office once, get him to read his work, thinking he'd help him out because he was another border writer, but he'd blown Roberto off because he wasn't a student.

"There was only one decent story in all of *Del Río*," Roberto continued. "About some kid hiding under his mom's bed." He exhaled a large cloud of dense smoke. "And *The Lone Vaquero*." Roberto shook his head. "That is the worst book anyone has been paid to write."

Joan laughed. She'd never read *Del Río*, or *The Lone Vaquero*, but she liked Carlos. He was jaded, and sexy, and he walked the halls of the UT English department like a vampire, tall, with his black hair slicked back, carrying the constant weight of what he'd been hired to represent. He flattered Joan but was brutal in his honesty, told her when she was simply being lazy, told her she needed to grow up. When she'd email him a hastily written, sloppy excerpt of her novel, he'd remind her that being a writer was like being a surgeon; it was about cutting, revising, toiling, perfecting. While Joan never internalized the advice, she did start bothering him less. It had been several weeks since she'd last contacted him.

"I'm working on a story about my dad right now," Joan slurred. "I haven't actually written it yet, but I came up with a title the other day. It's called 'Who Wants to Be Alone on a Saturday Night?'"

"That is a great title," Roberto said.

"You're just saying that."

"No I'm not. It is very Raymond Carver."

"You think so? That's good. I love Carver. Especially his titles. Titles feel so important to stories, you know? I feel like so many titles these days are boring as fuck . . ."

Joan kept rambling that way for a while as Roberto watched her, no longer listening. He eventually stood up and came toward her, bent over and put his mouth on hers, stuck his tongue deep into her mouth, nearly licking the back of her throat. She was shocked into submission, and they made out like that for what seemed to be an hour, but was probably only a few minutes.

"I should go," Joan said, finally, and as he walked her to her car, he told her that he liked her, that he'd even broken an agreement he'd made with himself that night.

"What agreement?" asked Joan.

"I swore to myself that I'd never kiss a girl wearing a Beatles T-shirt," Roberto said. Joan didn't know what to make of that.

The next day at her internship, while proofreading a bill that would require proper burials for aborted fetuses, Joan wondered what the fuck she was doing with Roberto. She wasn't *that* attracted to him, she thought. He had a subtle, musty smell that reminded her of her father—a mixture of smoke and mothballs. She knew she would probably have sex with him, in an effort to get over her most recent breakup with an organ player from Nantucket. She used the term *breakup* loosely, seeing as Nate (the organist) had made it clear that they were "never really together." She thought of how tall Roberto was, much taller than Nate. Six foot four, with a large head of wild, wiry hair atop his lanky, soft, and slender frame. She thought of all the books Roberto had read and all the things he knew, all the wisdom he might impart on her. He would be a good distraction—a fantasy and an escape. Deciding it would be wrong to lead Roberto on, Joan sent him a text message telling him exactly that. "You are a fantasy and an escape," she wrote, followed by: "Do you have any STDs?"

"This chick," Roberto responded. "No, I don't."

On their first real date Joan wore a short black dress with red flowers, a red cardigan sweater, and Mary Jane heels. "I like your short dress," Roberto said, placing his hand on her lower back, moving it down toward her ass.

They walked along Red River to a metal bar called Head Hunters, which had devils and flames painted on the walls, where they got really drunk and watched girls dancing on the bar tops. Joan began putting dollar bills in the girls' bikinis, making lewd, sexist comments. She told Roberto she planned to vote for Mitt Romney in November, an attempt to test him, perhaps. Joan loved Mitt Romney—his stiff, robotic innocence, his sober, sparkling eyes. He was like the father Joan had never had but always wanted. Roberto laughed as if this were the funniest thing in the world. "I don't give a shit about that, lady," he said. He rubbed her knee with his gigantic hand.

A couple of hours later Joan came to, out of a blackout, naked on top of her covers, her calves resting on Roberto's shoulders. He was looking into her eyes through his thick lenses, a pained expression on his face, his lip curled in a way that disgusted her. He was driving his dick in and out of her, methodically, and now that she was conscious, she began her perfunctory moaning, even though she could barely feel a thing. Not that he was particularly small, she was simply too drunk, too numb; it felt like she was being fucked in a dentist chair, high on laughing gas, shot up all over with novocaine.

"You are a fantasy and an escape," she wrote, followed by: "Do you have any STDs?"

"You are a very beautiful woman," he said. "You have a beautiful body."

She reached forward and dug her nails into his chest, which was impossibly soft and covered with deep craters, even deeper than the ones that covered his face. His body had been ravaged by acne.

"Please don't talk to me," she said.

"I love you," he replied, and she slapped him across the face, so hard that it shocked them both. He kept his head turned to the side as if to accentuate the drama of the slap.

"No you fucking don't," Joan said.

"But I do."

"Don't tell me that shit," she said, so angry she could have cried. She closed her eyes and turned her head away from him, refusing to look at him for the rest of the night.

The next morning, Roberto was gone, but his spiral notebook sat on the floor by her bed, apparently forgotten. Hungover, Joan smoked a joint and read the notebook out loud to her roommate in the living room. The first page began,

"My name is Roberto Rosa and I was born in Matamoros, Mexico . . ." He went on to talk about his hometown, how there were no bookstores and how he learned to read on his own. How he had no friends growing up and nobody liked him because of his terrible skin. He said that books were the only thing he had to turn to. He didn't lose his virginity until he was in his midtwenties, after the acne cleared up, leaving behind his "terrible battle scars." He talked about making love to women; he liked to tell them how beautiful they were and whisper in their ears. He talked about his mother, still in Mexico, with a mysterious debilitating illness. He seemed to resent her for it. Reading the notebook, Joan was struck by Roberto's self-assured tone, his ability to define himself, to view himself through such a clear and objective lens.

When she forgot her underwear at his house, he'd wear it to work the next day, even the thongs.

"He kind of sounds like a narcissist," Joan's roommate said, after she finished reading.

"No," said Joan, feeling all of a sudden defensive. "He's just a writer. That's how they are."

Joan and Roberto became inseparable for the next several weeks. They went out drinking all the time, always returning to his house to smoke tons of weed and have brutal, passionate sex like Joan had never experienced. He'd tell her the whole time that she was beautiful, grabbing her neck as if to choke her, pulling her hair. When she forgot her underwear at his house, he'd wear it to work the next day, even the thongs. He sent her dirty text messages, telling her that he was wearing her underwear, that last night she shook like a freight train, or cried like a little baby lamb. He wasn't always sexual in his texts. Sometimes he quoted Dickens or Faulkner or Bukowski or Miller to her, whatever he was reading that day, and she'd wonder how the fuck he could read so many books so fast.

She asked him one day why he liked Charles Dickens so much.

"Because, lady. I can relate to a guy like that. He came from nothing, like me, and literature saved him."

"That's beautiful," Joan said, but she never read any Dickens, or any of the other books Roberto recommended.

One night while they were having sex Joan started her period and bled, thick and heavy, all over his erection and his gold palm tree bedding, cheap and wiry, sent from his ailing mother in Matamoros.

"I'm sorry," she said. "I'm so sorry."

"That's okay, lady," he said. "I like having your blood on me, it's more operatic that way."

He never washed the sheets after that, and the deep red stain stayed there for weeks, like a crime scene. Each time she saw it, Joan was filled with pride. He loves even the most repulsive parts of me, she bragged to her girlfriends. He sleeps on my discharge.

Each morning he woke up and smoked a big bowl and typed for thirty minutes while Joan lay on the stain and stared at the ceiling. He had gotten to the point where he wrote one scene a day. It was the only way he'd ever get this shit done, he said. He was working on a novella called *Bitter Texas Honey,* which Joan would read a year later as a PDF file, and would convince herself was about her. Appearing in Roberto's novella would make Joan feel important, as if she had contributed in some way to the world of literature, not as a writer herself, but as a muse. While Roberto had a few stories and poems online by then, she would still have nothing published. At least in this way, she'd tell herself, she had accomplished something.

Soon Joan decided that she was in love with Roberto, and she wanted to claim him as her own. She went over to his house to talk him into the idea.

"I just don't think I can do it anymore, I can't have sex with you anymore if there's no commitment."

Roberto became visibly agitated, standing up suddenly and pacing around. "Look around you, lady," he said. "Look at where I live. I can't even pay my bills! They are going to turn my electricity off any day now. I can't even put food in my fridge!" He opened his refrigerator to show her there was nothing.

"What does that have to do with anything?" Joan asked. "What does that have to do with me?"

"You can't do it anymore. I understand, lady. I respect that."

He escorted her quickly out the door, like a bouncer of a nightclub, through his backyard, past all the eclectic, rusty sculptures, the stolen road signs, the fence covered with graffiti.

"Let go of me," Joan said.

"You are a beautiful and talented woman," he said.

"Fuck you," said Joan. "I don't need you to walk me any farther."

"Okay," said Roberto, and he stood by the fence and watched as she got into her white BMW and drove away. Once she reached the first stop sign, she began sobbing desperately.

Two years later, Roberto had a book published by a crazy man in Chicago. It was a story cycle called *The Bloody Uprising of the Well-Read Mexicans.* He emailed Joan, now that they were on good terms, to share the news (Joan had made amends to Roberto, after attending an expensive spiritual retreat in Northern California, where she cradled a small brown pillow that was supposed to represent Roberto as a baby. Joan, now close to one year sober, decided that she would go to his book launch to show support. It was at Farewell Books, a shabby shop on the east side that would surely go out of business soon.

She purchased one of his books, a tiny hardback with a kid in a skunk suit smoking a cigarette on the cover. She asked him to sign it for her. He smiled and bent down to hug her. He was wearing gray slacks and a vest and a tie. She'd never seen him in this outfit.

"I'm so happy to see you," he said. "They're already signed."

"Oh," said Joan. She opened the cover and saw.

"Here, I'll sign yours again," said Roberto, and he wrote something else on the title page. She thanked him and took her seat, watching him mingle. He had so many friends. Minutes later Roberto stood in front of the room at the microphone, and everyone went silent.

"This microphone stand perfectly represents the story cycle I published," he said. Everybody laughed. The stand was falling apart, covered with duct tape.

"I'm in a room full of the most creative people I know," he said. The crowd swelled with pride. Joan thought: *Who the fuck are these people?*

"I'd like to thank everyone from the Michener Center," he said, "who have shown me so much, and opened so many doors."

Joan wondered when in the past two years Roberto had cozied up to the MFA program that he used to talk so much shit about.

"I owe this all to my beautiful fiancée," Roberto said. "Without her none of this would be possible."

He began to read from his book, and Joan scanned the crowd.

His beautiful fiancée.

His beautiful fiancée.

His beautiful fiancée.

Was it that skinny bitch over there? Her gaze fell upon a petite blonde with a pixie haircut. Weird eyelids, though, Joan noted. Joan had gained at least fifteen pounds since getting sober. Maybe twenty. She adjusted the top of her jeans, and sat up straighter in her seat. Her neck suddenly felt hot, and her chest buzzed with anxiety. He didn't have the kind of penis I like anyway, she told herself, over and over again. She looked straight ahead. Long and thin, like a snake in the desert. Who wanted a lifetime of that?

He thanked the room, which erupted in applause. Joan didn't say goodbye. She got the fuck out of Farewell Books and into her dirty Mazda hatchback, still loaded full with her dead mother's belongings. Joan had cleaned out the house in Houston two weeks before, after her mother suffered an aneurysm at the family ranch.

She drove down Cesar Chavez, past the freeway, to the Whole Foods in the nice part of town, where she was supposed to meet with a woman she didn't know whose daughter was dead. They'd met at an AA meeting somewhere. Joan couldn't remember when. Sitting outside, waiting for the woman, Joan was approached by a short man in gym clothes who asked her if she wanted to get a drink sometime. Joan told him that he was bold to ask, but she didn't drink. He was new to town, from New Zealand. She was a writer? He was a writer too! Well, a copywriter, mainly web content. He told her it was cool that she didn't drink. He was really into fitness and he didn't drink much either. Everything about him, Joan found repulsive— his steady job, his healthy habits, his earnest gaze. She gave him her phone number, and in that moment she knew she would die alone. 🜚

FACTORS

Lizards will on purpose sever their tails when in stressful or dangerous situations, an act known as autotomy from the Greek *auto* "self" and *tome* "severing" or self-amputation. Even after the tail is cast off, it goes on wriggling, hence distracting the lizard's attacker. The lizard can regenerate its tail in a few weeks. The new tail will contain cartilage rather than bone and vary distinctly, not only in color but in texture, compared to its earlier appearance. In humans, change in skin pigment and texture are due to disease rather than protective behavior. I heard of a South African woman who was once white but turned black over time. It wasn't the reptile genes calling but a condition known as hyperpigmentation. Her husband asked for a divorce and took off with their three children.

The only mammals that come close to regeneration are the African spiny mice. Upon capture they release their skin. Imagine a predator holding its prey only to realize seconds later that it has escaped leaving only its skin. The mice regrow their skin, hair follicles, glands, fur, and cartilage with little or no scarring. Organic surgery at its finest.

Empirical sources suggest that "lizards, whose tail is a major storage organ for accumulating reserves, will return to a discarded tail after the threat has passed, and eat it to recover the supplies." This makes me think that when we discarded our tails as Homo sapiens, we were supposed to swallow them in order to keep our reserves intact. We forgot a significant part of ritual and opened ourselves to disease, predators, and a weaker immune system. Strangely, while looking in the mirror, I notice some things have fallen off my body and I can't locate them on the floor. Others attach to me like textile fabrics in all the wrong places. They fracture my ego, and I must find consolation that these zones of weakness make me softer. I want to know more about the self-amputation act, free will and all, but the English dictionary corrects the word to autonomy: self-rule, independence, freedom, sovereignty, which surprisingly concern the lizards when they're shedding tails; compelled by their strong desire to remain free, safe, uneaten, untrapped, unconquerable, and not subdued in accordance with their survival manual.

WAITING FOR HAPPINESS

Dog knows when friend will come home
because each hour friend's smell pales,
air paring down the good smell
with its little diamond. It means I miss you
O I miss you, how hard it is to wait
for my happiness, and how good when
it arrives. Here we are in our bodies,
ripe as avocados, softer, brightening
with latencies like a hot, blue core
of electricity: our ankles knotted to our
calves by a thread, womb sparking
with watermelon seeds we swallowed
as children, the heart again badly hurt, trying
and failing. But it is almost five says
the dog. It is almost five.

ON
SUBTLETY

Meghan O'Gieblyn

THE BEST ESSAY EVER!!!!!!!

I.

In ancient Rome, there were certain fabrics so delicate and finely stitched they were called *subtilis*, literally "underwoven." The word—from which came the Old French *soutil* and the English *subtle*—often described the gossamer-like material that was used to make veils. I think of organza or the finest blends of silk chiffon, material that is opaque when gathered but sheer when stretched and translucent when held up to the light. Most wedding veils sold today use a special kind of tulle called "bridal illusion," a term I've always loved, as it calls attention to the odd abracadabra of the veil, an accoutrement that is designed to simultaneously reveal and conceal.

II.

Doris Lessing once complained that her novel *The Golden Notebook* was widely misinterpreted. For her, the story was about the theme of "breakdown," and how madness was a process of healing the self's divisions. She placed this theme in the center of the novel, in a section that shares the title of the book, which she assumed

would lead readers to understand that it was the cipher. Rather than making the theme explicit, she wanted to hint at it through the form of the novel itself, "to shape a book which would make its own comment, a wordless statement: to talk through the way it was shaped." But in the end, her efforts did not translate. "Nobody so much as noticed this central theme," she complains in the introduction to the 1973 edition. "Handing the manuscript to publisher and friends, I learned that I had written a tract about the sex war, and fast discovered that nothing I said then could change that diagnosis."

There are people, of course, who will argue that divergent readings are a sign of a work's complexity. But whenever I return to Lessing's account of her novel's reception, I can't help but hear a note of loneliness, one that echoes all those artists who have been woefully misunderstood: Lewis Carroll wrote *Alice's Adventures in Wonderland* as a protest against abstract math. Georgia O'Keeffe insisted that her paintings of poppies and irises were not meant to evoke female genitalia (flowers, her defenders keep pointing out, fruitlessly, are androgynous). Ray Bradbury once claimed at a UCLA lecture that his novel *Fahrenheit 451* was not about censorship, but the dangers of television. He was shouted out of the lecture hall. Nietzsche abhorred anti-Semitism, but when Hitler came across a copy of *Thus Spoke Zarathustra*, he interpreted the image of the "splendid blond beast" as a symbol of the Aryan race. One wonders what might have happened had Nietzsche simply written: "lion."

One wonders what might have happened had Nietzsche simply written: "lion."

III.

We say that things are subtle when they are understated—such as makeup, or lighting—or when they are capable of making fine distinctions, as in a subtle mind. But the connotation of subtlety that has long preoccupied me is that which means "indirect" or "concealed," and also its archaic definition ("cunning, crafty"), which still haunts the contemporary meaning. "All literature is made of tricks," Jorge Luis Borges once said. Some tricks, he noted, are easy enough to decipher, but the best ones are so sly they hardly feel like tricks at all. As a child homeschooled in an evangelical family, left to my own devices for great swaths of time, I became particularly good at uncovering the most obvious cues in a text. I knew that the poet meant for snow to symbolize death, or that a conversation between two people concerned abortion, even though the story never used the word. Literary interpretation is, essentially, a form of hermeneutics—a skill one learns osmotically from listening to sermons, a genre in which I was immersed. But the stories that captivated and unsettled me were those that remained irreducible. In these, there were no codes to be cracked, no definitive meaning to be exposed—just the faintest sense that the surface of the text was undergirded by a vast system of roots that must remain forever invisible.

Today, many of the smartest people I know have become infatuated with melodrama, genre fiction, and TV dramas: narratives that wear their ideas easily on their sleeve. "It is heavy-handed in the best way," writes a prominent magazine critic about a novel that has recently been serialized for television. "It makes everything blunter and more explicit, almost pulpy at times." It seems that all of us, exhausted by New Criticism, caught up in the throes of peak TV, have finally outgrown whatever charms the elusive once held. There exists among people my age a tendency to dismiss subtlety as "evasive" or "coy," as though whatever someone has taken pains to conceal must be somehow ill intentioned, cut from the same unwholesome cloth as dog-whistle politics and the silky doublespeak of reptiles like Richard Spencer. Perhaps the slogans of the Trump era have now extended themselves to the arts: we must speak in one voice, in no uncertain terms. Each week, I receive emails from any number of activist organizations that begin in more or less the same way: "Let me be clear . . ."

Perhaps the slogans of the Trump era have now extended themselves to the arts: we must speak in one voice, in no uncertain terms.

IV.

For me, growing up in a Christian family required an interpretive vigilance, a willingness to harken to whispers. As children, we were taught to remain alert at all times. God could speak to you through a fortune cookie, a highway billboard, the lyrics of pop songs. Fools could proclaim his wisdom and radio DJs could be his angels in disguise.

Once, during a long drive to a church retreat, our youth pastor pointed to the license plate of the car ahead of us and explained that each of its letters corresponded to a problem he'd been praying over for months. Interpretation slid easily into paranoia and faith into superstition, but the point was you had to pay attention. If you let your guard down you might miss the miracle, like the disciples at Gethsemane who fell asleep on their watch.

The problem was you could never be certain the signs were not from the darker forces. The devil too was subtle, according to the book of Genesis: "Now the serpent was more subtle than any beast of the field which the Lord God had made." (My mother, who dictated the passages my siblings and I committed to memory, preferred the King James Version, which renders it *subtil*.) As a child, I often wondered what it meant that the devil was subtle. It was clear that he was mutable, appearing and disappearing throughout scripture in various disguises: as a snake, a lion, or an angel of light. More likely, though, it referred to his rhetoric, which was coy and Socratic: "Hath God said, Ye shall not eat of every tree of the garden?" A cruder entity would have made demands or arguments, but Lucifer wove elaborate traps of questions, prodding his victim to reach the relevant conclusion herself.

When I began writing, I believed that fiction should be a form of seduction. I wanted to write stories that were like the stories I loved: oblique in their approach, buttressed by themes that revealed themselves upon multiple readings. But in workshops, my classmates were vocal about the many problems lurking in my stories: the character's motivation was not clear; the backstory should be addressed, not alluded to; the conclusion was too cryptic. For a while, I dismissed this as obtuseness. People wanted things spelled out. They weren't reading closely. But there comes a point when a reproach is repeated so often it become impossible to dismiss. At times, it seemed less a critique of my craft than an indictment of my character. People regarded my tactics as cagey, as though I were ashamed of my ideas and trying to hide them behind a veil. More than once, readers discovered a meaning I hadn't intended. For a while, everything I wrote seemed to hazard misinterpretation, inviting accusations of chicanery, purposelessness, or bad faith.

V.

Christ himself was a master of the indirect, speaking in parables more often than sermons. In their original form, as they appear in the logia—the collection of his sayings that circulated before the writing of the gospels—the parables have the tenor of a riddle: A sower went out with a handful of seeds, scattering them across the earth. Some seeds fell on rocky soil, others fell on thorns, some were eaten up by birds before they could take root, but some found good soil and produced fruit. What does it mean? In the logia, Christ provides no guidance. Many of the stories end with the phrase "He who has ears, let him hear." Another riddle, though most scholars believe it to mean: Let he who is capable of understanding these mysteries receive them.

When I was at Bible school, struggling with the first shadows of doubt, the subtlety of the gospel troubled me. The message of salvation should have been democratic, available to all. But it was not clear. Time and again, the disciples asked Jesus if he was the son of God, and he refused to answer— or else gave some impossible reply: "Who do you say I am?" Was it not irresponsible that Christ had come to earth with a handful of koans and esoteric stories and expected his message to be understood by the entire world? I once raised this question in a theology course. The professor opened the question to the class. When it became clear that nobody was going to answer, he took off his glasses and spoke with a quiet gravity. "One paradox has remained true throughout history," he said. "The more explicitly God reveals himself to mankind, the more likely we are to reject him. Christ did finally declare himself the son of God, and we crucified him."

VI.

For as long as I can remember, I've had vivid and memorable dreams. They are often very beautiful, rendered in lush floral colors and almost cinematic in their level of detail. The only problem is that they are so relentlessly on the nose. When I turned thirty and my inbox was suddenly flooded with birth announcements, I had a recurring dream in which a tiny deformed man followed me around as I performed my daily rituals. I would be trying to brush my teeth, or walking to the store, and there was the little man waddling after me, waving amiably like a salesman trying to get my attention, so that I was forced to admonish him, beneath my breath, to go away. Another time, after I'd written something of which I was ashamed, I dreamt that I was sitting in my mother's kitchen being made to drink a vial of ink just as I'd been made to take cold medicine as a child. "Your dreams," my sister remarked once, "are like Freud for idiots."

If the purpose of dreams is to alert the conscious mind to what it has ignored or forgotten, then mine are very efficient—a fact for which I suppose I should be grateful. But I often wonder whether my subconscious isn't giving me too little credit. It is a strange thing to have your sensibilities so offended by your own dormant imagination. In the end, the obviousness of these messages makes me reluctant to heed them, as though doing so would only increase the grimy indignity of being pandered to.

VII.

During those years of doubt, when God seemed distant or completely silent, I tried to remind myself that this was what it meant to be the bride of Christ. Earthly life was imbued with a kind of romantic tension; it was a cosmic game of seduction wherein our creator played hard to get. If life seemed unjust, if God himself felt absent, it was because we were blinded, as humans, from seeing the unifying story that would emerge only at the end of time. Until that glorious wedding day, when the veil would be lifted and the truth would be revealed, the nature of reality must appear to us as shadows, like figures passing darkly across a clouded mirror.

When I finally abandoned my faith, I believed I was leaving this inscrutable world behind. I imagined myself exiting a primitive cave and striding onto terra firma, embracing a world where there would be no more shadows, no more distant echoes, only the blinding and unambiguous light of science and reason. But as it turns out, the material world is every bit as elusive as the superstitions I left behind. The laws of physics are slippery, and resistant to grand unifying theories. The outcomes of quantum experiments change depending on our observation of them. Particles solidify when we probe them, but become waves when we turn our backs. As the physicist Paul Davies once put it, "Nature seems to play tricks on us." Some scientists have now begun to take seriously the proposition that we exist within a multiverse, that we are forever separated from the truth of our existence by an impenetrable quantum veil.

What to make of this sly and nonsensical world that is indifferent to our curiosity? If the universe were a novel, we might say that it is "elusive," or perhaps even "opaque." If it were a god, we could only conclude that he had hidden his face. But perhaps it is a mistake—one common in our age of transparency—to perceive that which escapes our understanding as necessarily malicious. Others have found in these cosmic mysteries not tricks but signs of the ineffable. "The Lord God is subtle, but malicious he is not," said Albert Einstein. "Nature hides her secrets because of her essential loftiness, but not by means of ruse."

VIII.

I worry, once again, that my oblique approach has managed only to muddle things. I suppose I've been trying to suggest that subtlety is always a sign of mystery, and that our attitude toward the former is roughly commensurate to our tolerance for the latter. I have come to regard it as something of a dark art, a force of nature that can be summoned but never fully harnessed,

and can backfire at the slightest misstep. Anyone can pick up a bullhorn and make her intent clear to all, but to attempt something subtle is to step blindfolded into the unknown. You are always teetering on the brink of insanity. You are always walking on a wire strung across an abyss, hoping to make it from one end to the other without losing your balance, or your mind.

Perhaps this is another way of saying that subtlety is a transaction of faith. The artist must have faith that the effects will be perceived in the way she intends; the reader must trust that what he detects beneath the surface of the text is not merely a figment of his imagination. The disciple must come to believe that the whispers he hears in the wilderness are not the wind, or the devil, but the voice of his creator—just as the physicist must accept that there is order to the universe, even when its rules elude us. Such leaps of faith can be motivated only by love—a love so fierce it is willing to subsist on morsels, taking bread crumbs for a path in the dark. And perhaps, in the end, it is love that allows us to endure these mysteries, to subsist on so little, believing that somewhere, beyond the darkness, exists another consciousness that is trying to reach us. ◈

Ira Sadoff

THE DEFEAT OF BROOKLYN

I'm white inside, but that don't help my case
'cause I can't hide what is on my face
　　　　—LOUIS ARMSTRONG, "Black and Blue"

George Washington and I were dining at the inn after the defeat of Brooklyn.
He was a mopey little icon, the object of some scrutiny.
Since his lips were pursed I couldn't tell if his teeth were made of wood.
I tried to cheer him up with talk of America's future: Couldn't he hear
the ka-ching ringing from the skies? Soon we'd be all hope
and avarice, our troops overseas, our little hamburgers everywhere.

When Washington decreed no black could fight in his army,
he had no idea I was black. I mean inside out, which is what we white people think,
for we too had been beaten, have been slaves to buying and selling, we too
hated our masters, whether they were bankers
or trustees of the court. That's the case I was making, because *liar*,
appropriator, *solipsist*, *out of our hands*, these were the lessons

we took from homeschooling. A thousand men left for dead. The army
split in two, and—just so you know—next time you sit
in Battery Park staring at women's butts, you might want to thank Washington
for knocking off some of your ancestors (before you go back to the office).
Lunch hour was almost over, and we were both in a black mood,
which made drinking together easy. When I got up to pee

I thought to myself this guy's so famous no one will remember me
unless I snap the two of us together. We of the same country.

BIOGRAPHICAL SKETCH

I've been a soft touch, a rough ride, I took shots
at congressmen, left an outrageous tip
for a waif whose hand was shaking

as she poured my tea. I made the sound of a wolf
in Naomi's bedroom, was shabby
at her wedding, sulking

while pinning an amorous note
to her gown. I refused to cross a picket line
then bought a handsome silk shirt

sewn in the most downtrodden district in China.
This when I was learning how to be a person,
which right now's an unfinished symphony.

But when I think of Mozart on his deathbed,
penning his own requiem, I can't abide my irony.
Nobody warned me about the solemn passages,

when we know no one, when we could die
far from home with our bungled furies and crushes
yammering beside us: *Not yet, not yet.*

NEW VOICE FICTION

I Have Her Memories Now

Carrie Grinstead

I went to grade school with Marlie O'Hagan, the world's first recipient of a double-organ transplant. I despised her. As a toddler, she'd suffered three heart attacks, and lived only because a surgeon had figured out how to cut the heart and liver from a dead child and sew them inside her.

Marlie was a miracle of modern medicine, Mother said. Marlie was always in the newspaper, and Mother liked to show me the pictures and read the stories aloud. In my nightmares, before I even met her, Marlie sat before a roaring fire, eating pale flesh from a plate. I tried to scurry away but only scurried in place. Marlie peeled my skin back with her fingers and licked my blood gently.

On the first day of kindergarten, a reporter crouched on the blacktop, holding a microphone to Marlie's mouth. Mother and I joined a wide half circle of spectators who applauded every time Marlie spoke. She was smaller than I expected, her wispy hair a brighter orange. Built like a teddy bear, with a puffy round face and protruding tummy to match. Beneath her eyes, wormy yellow scars marked the places where cholesterol once bulged through her skin. Soft fur covered her face and arms and glittered gold in the light of morning.

Fur! I pawed frantically at Mother's purse. "Why—" I gasped. Why, why, why. Mother swatted my shoulder and hissed, "Be quiet! Be nice!"

Marlie tilted her head in my direction and smiled crookedly, sleepily, as if she'd just been roused from the grave. I spewed a rainbow of cereal across the parking lot, and the reporter glanced at me and laughed.

• • •

I, too, was a miracle. Because of modern medicine, Mother didn't need a man to have a family. Alone, her body had created life, pulsing legs and kicking heart, hands to grasp and mouth to eat. In my earliest years she held me while the days closed over our little house. She touched me toe by toe. She smiled to make me smile.

Mother held me in the living room with the long-cold fireplace. Mother held me in her bedroom, where shoe boxes hid treasures: my footprints and a lock of my hair, dried flowers, notes too faded to read. Endless clippings from the newspaper. Mother held me in the doorway that opened to our untended garden. Crickets trilled, and ferns curled along the fence, in the shade of a neighbor's maple tree. A cluster of purple coneflowers persisted, year after year.

. . .

Marlie gave off a stale, sweet smell that overpowered the crayons and glue and snot in our kindergarten classroom. Her voice was raspy like my chain-smoking uncle's. She was dumb, couldn't learn her letters, and was constantly falling asleep. Yet the teacher fussed over her, and she always got to take our classroom hamster home on weekends.

> In my nightmares, before I even met her, Marlie sat before a roaring fire, eating pale flesh from a plate.

In my dreams, she ate him.

Our classmates liked her well enough. The ones who took gymnastics lessons made a big production out of treating her like any other girl. Fat kids and nose-pickers loved to pet her arms and ask her to lift her shirt and show her surgical scars. I was disgusted by this, and fascinated. I hated and feared Marlie, but in my own way I was as obsessed as Mother. I wanted to forget the scars, and I wanted to touch the scars. I wanted to peel their edges loose with my fingernails.

I made no friends at school, and I was neither praised nor punished. I sang at moderate volume and colored acceptable hand puppets. I ran wild on the playground. A flip over the monkey bars, a dash across the balance beam, a twirl in the middle of the wood chips. Never more than a few seconds in one place, lest anyone try to play with me, never an instant of stillness, lest I draw the attention of playground monitors. The teacher told Mother I was doing fine, just fine, no problems, fine, and Mother said, "What is that supposed to mean? Does she even know who you are?"

She didn't, and I successfully avoided everyone until Halloween, when Mother sent me to school with twenty pieces of off-brand chocolate taped to greeting cards. We drew ghosts and headstones on paper bags, then raced around the classroom screaming, "Trick or treat!" in each other's faces and spilling fruit punch all over ourselves. We might as well have been a swarm of flies, for all anyone noticed anyone else, but I was careful even so. When Marlie was by the cubbies, I veered to the door. When Marlie fed candy corn to the hamster, I crawled under a table. I moved in constant opposition to her, even at the cost of the good candy that the gymnasts had brought. But I made the fatal error of sitting at the table to rest from my efforts. A green-mittened hand landed on my shoulder. A sick chill shot to the base of my stomach.

"I like your costume," Marlie said.

I was a doctor. I wore a stethoscope and a lab coat that hung to my ankles. A stupid costume, Mother's idea, and of course, of course she'd put me in it knowing it would attract Marlie. I wanted to scream, but tears clogged my throat. Helplessly, I turned.

> In moments like these, the whole world tilted sideways.

Marlie was a perfect frog. Green footie pajamas trapped and strengthened her sweet smell until it was almost sour. A pink fabric tongue with a plastic fly glued to it hung by a safety pin from her collar. The hood, plush, with round eyes on top, was store-bought, and her mom had even painted her face green. The makeup had flaked away from her scars and formed clumps in her fur. It was gross but effective, and for an instant, impossibly, I was happy. We were small and weedy together, at the edge of a pond in summer.

"You even sound like a frog," I whispered.

Marlie smiled in that way she had, her mouth simply a hole that fell open, the corners of her eyes flickering as if she didn't actually know whether or not she was happy. She drew a high, hesitant breath. "It's because of my medicine," she said.

"Okay," I choked, and the closing bell released me.

• • •

Reporters and photographers came often to our school, and it pissed Mother off royally that I was never in pictures with Marlie, never one of Marlie's little friends who said, "She's really just like any other girl," and got their names printed in the paper. All through the dark winter, she'd charge into my bedroom with the latest story in hand, wanting to know why I didn't tug the reporter's sleeve and make a comment. "Don't you play with Marlie?" Mother would ask. "Isn't Marlie your friend?" No, no, no, I'd answer, and she'd pull me out of bed and make me practice tugging her sleeve.

After our garden melted into a spring swamp, Mother grew tired of fighting me and decided it was the reporters' fault. Why didn't they give everyone an equal chance? What, exactly, did they find wrong with Mother's daughter?

. . .

In first grade, we were visited by a big-bottomed lady reporter from Philadelphia. Sitting in one of our chairs in the back of the classroom, she looked like she was hovering in air. She caught me staring, pursed her lips, and winked, as if to remind me of all the things she knew and I didn't.

During the midmorning milk break, she sang "Baby Beluga" with us and swayed side to side. Marlie, seated beside her, sometimes didn't sway fast enough and got brushed in the head by the reporter's drifting boob. A grown lady acting like a child, a big person pretending to be small. A dead girl living. A dead girl singing. In moments like these, the whole world tilted sideways.

. . .

In third grade, just after Thanksgiving, Marlie was on the cover of *People* magazine. Reporters had followed her for a week and taken glossy pictures of Marlie eating a plate of Lit'l Smokies, Marlie playing four square at recess, Marlie at her desk with her chin in her hand. "Look!" Mother cried, as she paced the living room and I ate SpaghettiOs in front of the TV. "Look, it's you!" She thrust the magazine between me and my bowl. Our classroom filled half a page, and I remembered the day. Way back when I could still walk to school without a jacket, when sunlight washed seedlings in the classroom window sills. Marlie, in the foreground of the picture, selected a book from the Accelerated Reader shelf. Three gymnasts crowded together on a beanbag chair. A boy, grinning like an idiot, leaned sideways in his desk to get in range of the camera. Just beyond him, off in a corner, I peered into my desk. The afternoon before, I'd been detained after school and made to take everything out, scrub away pencil shavings, dried glue, and bits of my fingernails, and put my school supplies back in neatly. On that morning, the blue notebook I'd placed on top was a jewel in the sun. It filled my vision, stilled my heart. By Thanksgiving it was once again buried in the unholy mess of my desk. Mother showed me the picture, and I felt a pang of longing, but I said, "Yeah, so?" and slipped the tip of my tongue through an O.

Mother followed me around the house, reading the story. Marlie worked with a tutor every day after school. Marlie liked to play catch with her dad and help her mom in the kitchen. When Marlie grew up, she wanted to write a book called *In the Darkness*. It would be about the things she thought of while lying awake at night, and about all the pets she'd had.

"Isn't that the sweetest thing?" Mother gasped.

Then Mother had an idea. "I'm a mom too," she declared. "There's no reason I can't call another mom and set up a sleepover."

I cried, I pleaded, but two nights later Marlie showed up at our house with her pajamas in a pillowcase. We ate pea soup and watched *The Facts of Life*. Marlie sang the theme song, and her rasping voice loosened my teeth from their sockets. I pressed my hands to my ears, squeezed my eyes shut, and begged, "Shut up! Will you please shut up!"

When I opened my eyes, Marlie was fiddling with a bit of loose carpet and staring mildly at the TV. "How come you never talk?" she said. "We can talk about school if you want."

Mother brought pillows and blankets into the living room. "This will be fun! When I was a little girl, I loved camping out in the living room."

Fun was not really the reason; the reason was that my bedroom, intended as a storage closet, was big enough for a twin bed and a bureau but little else. Still, I accepted Mother's living room camp-out plan, and pretended it was fun, because as soon as Mother went to her room I would make a break for mine. I would close the door, hide deep under the covers, and forget that Marlie O'Hagan was in my house.

Mother spread a quilt across the carpet. She propped two pillows against the hearth and patted them vigorously. "There! Perfect! A nice little bed. You girls get tucked in, and I'll read you a story."

I snorted as she left the room. When did Mother ever read anything but the paper? Was she going to read Marlie a story about herself?

Mother returned with a large green volume, *Elves, Fairies, and Other Little People*, a book I'd often admired at the mall. It contained lush drawings of fauns hiding among riverbank rushes, a list of worldwide elf sightings, and details of leprechaun behavior. It had no stories, and Mother would have known that if she'd bothered to open it before buying it. Oh Mother, Mother, Mother, with her thinning hair and hollow eyes. She thought she knew me because she'd made me. She thought she was sophisticated because she owned a little house. She thought we were special because a miracle girl lived in our town.

Marlie slipped politely beneath the covers. I sat on the hearth. Mother laughed. "What are you doing? Get in bed."

"I want to sit here."

"What are you talking about? It's cold and hard there! Get in your nice warm bed with your friend."

Marlie lay patiently on her back, furry arms resting above the blankets. I shook my head, and Mother tugged me away from the hearth. "No!" I screamed. I kicked and struggled, tangling the blankets. Mother, stronger than she looked, pushed my shoulders and got me down on one knee. I dropped low, rolled free, and ran for the bathroom. Mother caught me by the ankle, and I fell headlong into the hallway. I curled into a tight ball, but Mother pursued her advantage and pried me open. She pinned my shoulders to the floor and clamped my hips between her knees. She blocked out the ceiling light, and into her darkness I shrieked, "I don't want to feel the fur!"

Oh Mother, Mother, Mother. She thought she knew me because she'd made me.

Mother gave a single sharp gasp. She leaned closer, closer, until her narrow nose and disbelieving mouth hovered inches from mine. Her breath smelled empty as snow. "That's mean! That's shallow! That girl has already suffered so much."

Mother would have talked on if I'd let her, stacked argument on top of argument until I could no longer see. I gritted my teeth and cried, "She's a monster! I hate her!" with such force that Mother tilted back, loosening her legs just enough for me to crawl free. I scrambled to the bathroom.

"Fine!" Mother screamed. "Nice girls get to listen to bedtime stories! Mean girls don't."

Icy air leaked around the edges of the bathroom window. Pipes in the walls thudded. I wrapped myself in towels, swallowed hard, and imagined myself down into my neck. Down once more to a warmer, darker place, where pulses were thick as summer air in our garden, on days when neighbors spread mulch.

Marlie tapped the bathroom door, and without thinking I tumbled back into the light and let her in. "I have to go to the bathroom," she said.

Towel around my shoulders, I sat on the edge of the tub while she washed her hands. She stood on her toes to reach the sink. At the back of the bathroom closet was a stepping stool I'd used in years past. I thought about the stool and about the years: the sink filled with hot water on the shortest days of December, my hands submerged; my breath fogging the mirror as I worked a loose tooth.

Marlie yelled at me to go away, and gymnasts called me a creep, but I lived among the parts and pieces of the body.

Droplets clung to Marlie's fur and shimmered under the vanity's bare bulb. "You have hair too," she said. "Are you a monster?" She left the water running while she pumped soap. A single, dainty drop, and, oh, Mother would have loved that! She was always insisting one pump was plenty and telling me I needed to stop filling my whole palm, unless I had my own personal soap money. Lately, she was trying to convince me to at least cut the amount by half, a compromise I was considering.

Marlie scrubbed and rinsed. "My cyclosporine makes my hair grow like this. I have to take it to protect my organs. If I didn't I would die. So I have more hair than you. So what. I don't care what you think." She closed the tap and dropped back down to her heels. "I hate you too," she said.

· · ·

A week later, during library time, I requested a book about cyclosporine. "Is that a person?" the librarian asked. "It's for organs," I said, and she gave me a heavy book with illustrations of a liver in cross section, a fetus in utero, and capillaries magnified ten thousand times. On the due date, I hid the book under my mattress and claimed it was lost. Mother paid the replacement cost and grounded me until New Year's.

The joke was on her, because I had no friends and nowhere to go, nowhere I wanted to be except my closet room. Wedged between bed and bureau, I studied the book in lamplight, lost all sense of place and time in the two-page spread of the liver. Veins appeared as holes pocking a land-scape of tightly packed pink cells. Funny words twisted around my tongue. *Canaliculi. Fenestration.* Little red cells darted now here, now there. Great hills called lobules rose into a dusty sky.

All of this inside me! I winced in disbelief, laughed in disgust. For days, I thought of nothing but the glomerulus, a squirming ball of capillaries inside my kidney. At school, Marlie yelled at me to go away, and gymnasts called me a creep, but I lived among the parts and pieces of the body.

One of my favorite pictures, the skin at six hundred times' magnifica-tion, inspired me to experiment in the bathroom with Mother's leg-shav-ing razor. I shaved off thin white ghosts of my fingerprints and squeezed out perfect red beads. I learned to control the flow with tourniquets fash-ioned from hair ties. I leaned close, I squinted. I never gave up hope of seeing the platelets and the fibrin net.

I loved the progress of scabs. I scraped them with scissors as they changed from red to purple to yellow. I saved the bits in sandwich bags or sprinkled them over snow.

· · ·

In the spring of fifth grade, Marlie's surgeon, her miracle worker, came to Career Day. Streets and buildings in Pittsburgh already bore his name, and reporters from all over the state joined the fifth- and sixth-grade classes in the gym. We sat on the floor, reporters and teachers lined the walls, and Dr. Marrona's stool was on a riser set up under the basketball hoop. Marlie sat there with him and held Muffin, a fourteen-year-old pug who had sur-vived his double-organ transplant three years before Marlie got hers.

Dr. Marrona was the tallest man I'd ever seen and the first man I ever loved. He wore striped linen slacks that made him look a little like the sous chef who'd spoken to us earlier, and a lot like a pirate. He sat as if he'd fallen onto the stool from a height, legs angled out, back hinged forward, shoulders hunched. He spoke in a low rumble and didn't seem to realize he was talking to children. Our teacher asked, "Did you know when you met Marlie that she was the one? Could you tell she had the spirit to make it through?"

"No," he said. "It took us thirty years to figure out organ rejection, and a lot of people died along the way. A lot of dogs too. There was nothing wrong with their spirit."

Cameras flashed. Muffin shivered in Marlie's lap. A sixth-grade teacher launched into a rambling question that had something to do with the body as a house: "The way I like to think of it is, the blood vessels are hallways, and organs are bedrooms."

I rolled my eyes up. Sometimes the sixth-grade boys' basketball team threw balls so hard and high that they looped over the blades of the ceiling fans. I loved that.

"If you look at pictures of the lining of the intestines," the sixth-grade teacher said, "it even looks like carpeting."

A lonely smile broke slowly across Dr. Marrona's face. "My first-year anatomy and physiology professor used to say metaphors would screw you over, every time." He lifted a stack of index cards in the teachers' direction. "Did you want me to talk about being a surgeon?" He tapped the index cards on his knee. "Training will take you at least ten years. It took me fourteen."

Other speakers that day had been for everyone else: the long-haul trucker who owned shot glasses from each of the lower forty-eight states; the sous chef who made us all sing about sauces; the radio DJ who once interviewed Cyndi Lauper.

Dr. Marrona was for me. He hunched further into himself and seemed to be in private conversation with his index cards as he said, "I knew guys who were incredible memorizers. Blew me out of the water in those early A and P classes. But all that really matters is the first time you operate on a live animal. Some guys hit the floor as soon as blood touched their gloves."

I would not hit the floor. I would journey through veins, navigate thick warrens of lesser vessels, brave rivers of bile until lobules rose before me. Dr. Marrona would teach me to cut out, sew in, make the monsters, perform the miracles.

He lowered the index cards to his thigh. "I'll say this about being a surgeon. People really will love you. More than they should." He turned to Marlie. "Marlie's donor—I certainly didn't do anything for that little girl. But every year on her birthday I get a card from her mother."

Marlie shook her head frantically. She said, "But you did!" and up there on the riser she was a tiny, distant flash of light. Dr. Marrona gave her the microphone, and she gripped it with both hands. "You did do something!" she cried. "I have her memories now. I remember somebody else's house and somebody else's parents. I remember the car seat and the white sky and the tires whispering across ice."

The gym was startled into silence, and for that I loved Marlie. Teachers stood with jaws unhinged. Cameras hung stupidly around photographers' necks. Laughter rolled up from my stomach and was just about to exit my mouth when the gym dissolved into chaos. Kids talked at once, reporters screamed questions, and photographers tried to get one last shot as Dr. Marrona, Marlie, and Muffin exited through a side door.

I ducked out the back, catching up to them in the hall. Tiny Marlie, giant Dr. Marrona, Muffin in harness behind them, jolting a bit with every step as if the floor were electrified.

I followed them outside, slipping through the heavy metal door just before it closed. Marlie carried Muffin down the concrete steps to the parking lot and set him near a grassy crack in the black-top. Muffin was too frail to hold himself up while arching his back to do his business. Dr. Marrona leaned down, down, down and helped him by holding the harness. Marlie said, "Good boy, Muffin. Good boy."

"You did this to yourself?" he asked, and my heart beat until there was no room for breath. I nodded.

I waited at the top of the steps, but they didn't see me. Marlie looked right through me and made me wonder for an instant if I were dreaming, or dead. Dr. Marrona drew a bag from the pocket of his striped pants. I walked down one step, down three. "Hi," I said. Louder: "Hi."

He returned to his full height, and his shadow fell over me. "Hello," he said.

"I want to be a surgeon! I can operate. I won't hit the floor." I held out my hands, the crisscrossing, oozing, scarring proof of my efforts. He took them in one of his, cupping them like baby birds.

"You did this to yourself?" he asked, and my heart beat until there was no room for breath. I nodded. "You like doing it? Is it fun for you?"

"Yes," I whispered. Fun, sure. *Fun* was one word. Fun was one piece of those hours in the bathroom, when I planned my cuts and tried to control my blood and skin.

"I don't like it," Dr. Marrona said. "It scares the hell out of me. If you think it's fun then I wouldn't want you operating on me, or on anybody I care about."

Marlie tugged his sleeve, and he scooped her up in his arms. Washed in sun and sky and birdsong, she cuddled into his shoulder. He kissed her furry forehead and rested his nose in her orange hair.

"She can't be a surgeon," Marlie told him. "She's too mean."

. . .

Career Day went on. I breathed. I clapped politely. I walked home. I digested the noodles Mother set in front of me. I dreamed of light, stupid things that left me hollow all through the next day.

On the weekend, I hid beneath my blanket and cried. I didn't cry over Dr. Marrona's words to me, which shimmered in a corner of my mind, too bright to look at. Marlie's comment I dealt with easily enough: I stoked my hate and burned her opinion to dust. I cried because fourteen years was longer than I'd been alive. If I started my training immediately (and I wouldn't start immediately, because Dr. Marrona did not want me), I would still be twenty-five before I became a surgeon. Impossibly old. Surely I didn't need fourteen years, or even ten. I already knew the difference between veins and arteries. I could spell *hepatocyte* and label every organ of the abdomen.

The door of our house swung open, swung closed, and Mother went out into the melting snow to do the things she did. Talk to the men smoking cigarettes outside the grocery store, buy the newspaper and the SpaghettiOs. I retrieved a paring knife from the kitchen. In the bathroom, I sat on the edge of the tub and imagined Marlie's scars onto my belly. Hip to hip, tracing the curve between ribs and stomach.

I was smart and I was steady, but the skin was thick. It resisted, and it hurt. I stabbed, without success. I wanted to open the right side, where my liver was, but it was easier to reach across my body and work from the left. I drew blood, at last, through persistence rather than force. I scraped and scraped with the knife's tip until red dots appeared, and then I had holes to widen.

I made a good, deep cut, and blood surged down onto my underpants. I should have been somewhere in range of my left kidney, and when I saw no sign of it I felt the first rush of fear. Outside, gray clouds moved between sun and window. The blood that gloved my hands turned from bright red to purple. I pressed. I dug. I expected the blood to stop and give me a clearer space to work. I expected the dizziness to stop; I knew a person didn't die when the belly was opened, because Marlie's had been and she was still alive—but it seemed I was dying. I would never be able to explain to Mother that it was an accident.

Tears coursed down my face. They flowed without sobs, without help from me. When Mother came home she must have sensed it all through smell or instinct. She dropped her grocery bags in the doorway, ran down the hall, and, screaming, threw open the door.

. . .

That night, a dumpy man repaired my cut with twenty-three stitches. I hadn't even breached the deep layers of the skin, let alone the fat and fascia and peritoneum. Still, my attempt at self-surgery was enough to earn me a case report in a regional medical journal.

I spent ten days in a horrible place, where white-faced children screamed in the night and walked around with no laces in their shoes. In a room with creaking armchairs and flaccid teddy bears, Mother visited me. She always cried, but I didn't know if she was crying for me or for Marlie, whose new heart had stopped suddenly, late at night, one week after Career Day.

By the time I came home Mother herself had become a ghost. I'd leave for school in the morning while she was still in bed, and I'd come home to find her sitting on the floor, smoking and watching TV. For weeks, layers of grease formed on the kitchen counters, even though we never ate anything but cereal and the noodles I learned to boil. Some nights, after wiping the underside of the toilet seat or tugging a clot of hair from the tub drain, I went to bed tight with frustration because no notice, no praise ever came. But Mother, quiet and useless, frightened me, and I hid from her in the dust I brushed off the television and the school clothes I folded each evening.

On the last day of fifth grade, my heart rose as I turned up our sun-soaked street and saw that Mother had taken out the trash. But inside the can were shoe boxes full of Marlie's newspaper clippings.

I saved them all, kept them under my bed, and in the night Marlie rose from their depths. She sat naked on my bed, her golden fur growing until her scars were covered, growing and flowing to fill the room. Marlie opened her rib cage, removing organs one by one and lining them up on the bureau like precious toys.

I vacuumed our house. Once a month, I changed our sheets. When winter came again, I shoveled snow. I did the best I could, and I was nice. No one could ever accuse me otherwise. 🔹

THE ANESTHESIA OF ABSTRACTION

I.

Talk of oneness or twoness or the trinity,
of beingness or the Kingdom of God,
of love, presence, the numinous and eternal:
how far away such talk takes us, far away
from the shade of the avocado tree,
the thighs of ripe persimmon,
the tongues of cattle licking
the great blocks of salt
in a hot
dawning
field.

2.

For every time someone says systems theory
one must say pines in the darkness;
for every time someone says biodiversity
or biophilia or sustainability
someone must shout musk
or barracuda or the whiskers
of the carrot. The real, living,
piebald world: we drop a cloak over it
with our cumbrous sophistication.
For every time someone says
cumbrous sophistication
someone must say the thighs
of the goddess
stippled
with
light.

ON ODYSSEUS

The raider of cities,
the great-hearted hero,
the man skilled in all ways of contending,
the wiliest fighter of the islands,
the shrewd and royal and kingly man,
the champion, the old soldier, the noble and enduring man,
the man for all schemes and battles, the man for all occasions,
the man of ranging mind, double-minded, several-minded,
the one no one could touch for gallantry, craft, and gall,
Lord Odysseus of Ithaka, son of Laertes,
cries upwards of seventy-five times
over the course of Homer's retelling.
And I'm not talking sniffling a bit.
I'm talking weeping, keening, sobbing.
Unearthly lamentation. A man who,
again and again, *tastes his grief.*
"Oh Teddy," I say flipping through
the pages of the old book,
"there seems to be a lesson here."

TEMPLE EXAMPLE

The mind doesn't do what we want it to do.

Mine plays speed Scrabble; it sifts pages and pages

of pictures of shoes. Palmyra goodbye. Temple of Bel not a pun

but a ruin. A ruined ruin, a ruin sent to oblivion

on purpose. Who cares if I fold up at my desk

a heap of angry sorrow. Not any candidate,

no ambassador. Sign a petition? Email some senators?

I make nothing happen. I make

nothing but orders, seven-letter words, coffee

with the hard water from the oleander-pierced pipes

with their roaches and mud. A temple

stood for twenty centuries and today the *New York Times*

shows us its new life as dust. *Baal* is how they spell it.

A neat aerial square of nothing now. The world wants

what from us in reply to the hatred of the mind?

I should say "soul," I know, or "history" or "culture"

but probably only the mind can thwart destructions.

In America, the mind is also hated,

by whosoever sells us shoes and phones. We are subtle

here, give lots of money to the arts.

LEAVE NO TRACE

The boy went hiking for a month

he took his books

boots from Italy meant for Alps and weather

and with his friends 400 pounds

of food: lentils lentils lentils

quinoa! lentils

He left Coetzee's *Disgrace*

on a rock in the sun and hiked on

and then remembered two miles out

                  so two went back

He said they searched in case

the spot was misremembered

but the book was gone   two miles

to rejoin the resting others

Four extra miles that day

Three chapters in and so much

left to find out   everyone rolling

their eyes   Poor boy

poor ruffled book flickering in the wind

and then a swoop   pages as mild drag

against this mama hawk   swoop

swoop and then she's busy shredding

when her mate returns   stalks

or pine needles   husks   in his beak

homemaking   rough twiggy nest

as big as a small wheelbarrow

Softened now   the strips of pages

weathered and jostled and rumpled

and macerated (sort of) (beakily)

and in those pages   tucked and warm

two or three blue eggs

two or three speckled chests

and those bleating cries

Slide and Glide

Leigh Newman

M y wife, Meryl, was having an affair. All through our prep for the pear-and-gorgonzola salad, she kept trying to tell me about it—turning suddenly toward me at the cutting board, her face a blur of panic and determination.

Our friends were due at the house in twenty minutes. She dumped the pine nuts into the blender, then a bunch of limp parsley. As she reached for the garlic, she looked up at me as if it were the last time she might do so, which could have been my imagination, but probably wasn't.

A whoosh went through me, the way it does when your ski catches ice and skitters out from under you. I had a jug of corn oil in my hands and steadied myself by studying the happy yellow cob on the label.

"How could I forget olive oil?" said Meryl. "And the basil?"

I looked at her. She had gone to the store last week and stayed there for six hours. The bag she had brought back was mostly milk and bananas.

Into the blender went the corn oil—thin, industrial-colored—one cup, two cups, three, double what the recipe called for. And still I poured.

"Stop," said Meryl when I reached the lip of the pitcher. She broke off from my eyes, reached for the puree button. I grabbed her wrist. The doorbell rang in the background. Neither of us flinched.

"What if we got out of here?" I said. There was something hoarse and horrible in my voice, something that snuffed out the charming, disastrous husband I had been for most of our marriage, and all I could do was hope she would ignore it.

"The cabin!" I said, the idea coming to me as if it had been there all along. "We've never been out there in the winter."

"I don't know," she said, slowly, so slowly I wondered if my brain was still syrupy from the weed I'd smoked that afternoon. I imagined a jovial tone and tried to infuse it through my next sentence. "We should all go! Me, you, Jack, Conner! Everybody!"

There was a long, quiet stretch before she tilted her head, then asked, "How long would we be gone?" The sorrow in her voice bled through me, and despite the fury sparkling through my mind, as it had been for the past few weeks, growing harder and clearer and more comforting, despite the doorbell's insistent second ring, I understood that I would not grab her other wrist and shake the truth out of her. His name. How he had bought our groceries for her. How she had looked down at his anorexic bag and known that she would never leave a store without a bunch of Swiss chard or dried mango or the rest of the items on the list on our fridge, how she had known that I knew this about her.

And yet.

I hit the puree button. "A few days!" I said, over the crunch and spin of metal, the pesto silkening into liquid. "A few days at the cabin will be good for us—as a family."

> **I understood that I would not grab her other wrist and shake the truth out of her.**

• • •

There were six of us at the table. To my right sat Paulie D., my best friend since seventh grade. He was a broad, bearded fellow, a pediatric dentist, who, no matter what the season, smelled of woodsmoke and fluoride rinse. Every summer, he and his wife, Ginny, marched their four daughters up the peaks of the Wrangells and camped out for six weeks.

"You're a brave woman," he said to Meryl when I mentioned the trip to the cabin. "I don't do kids in the bush under ten."

The jambalaya went around, followed by a bowl of pasta and the corn-oil-parsley-pesto-glop. All of which Meryl let pass by, in favor of a fast, very full glass of Cab.

Janice, who was married to Neil, my other best friend from seventh grade, wondered about the ski to the cabin. Cross-country with a toddler was, well, exhausting.

"We'll use a sled," I said. "Conner can sit there. I'll pull him. Lots of people do it."

"You got a Kindersleigh?" said Janice.

Meryl glanced at me, her face disbelieving but also so heartbreakingly and openly hopeful that I had a Norwegian Kindersleigh, to the tune of three grand, hidden in some closet of our crappy split-level that still needed a new deck. She knew me so well . . . and still. I knew her so well . . . and still. Were these twin snowflakes of delusion the only reason we were even married—believing that one amazing day, either she or I would finally do something so unlike ourselves that we would finally make the other happy?

"Well," I said. "I never gave away Blackie's harness."

"Crappy Blackie!" said Ginny. "I miss that dog."

Laughs all around. I poured a glass of white and tried to keep the injured look off my face. Giving up Blackie was still a sore point for me, despite his many digestive issues and his habit of chewing on the kids' hands. I had brought him home as a surprise, thinking—stupidly—a puppy might help us.

> It was that kind of affair, when even the briefest separation makes your heart feel suctioned out of your chest.

The whole table chimed in with suggestions about the kind of sled I should use: A Flexible Flyer. A cafeteria tray! A lid from a garbage can! More laughs, even from Meryl.

"First off," I said, "I'd never put my son on a Flexible Flyer. They're too heavy and he can't sit on hard, bare wood that long. Second, I was going to use—"

"A plastic saucer," said Neil, quietly. "Light. Not unstable."

I could have hugged him. He and Janice lived down the street, in a log palace with one too many antler chandeliers. But of all of us, he was the master outdoorsman. Two summers ago, he had disassembled his helicopter, shipped it from Anchorage to Tunisia, reassembled it, and flew around the desert, hunting wild boar. Meryl thinks he is a nutcase. I think she grew up in Wisconsin, and mostly, we leave it at that.

"I thought I'd test out waxes on the bottom," I said.

"I'd go old school with a saucer," said Neil. "Soap it."

A kind of soft, contented quiet ensued during which I believed that he, Paulie, and I were all thinking the same thing, how our dads used to haul us out to the wilderness in rickety Super Cubs and rusted-out campers, leading us down rivers in some leaky raft borrowed from a guy at work.

Meryl looked up. "What if Jack won't listen?"

For a moment, there was only the sound of forks on plates as our friends glanced at each other, presumably remembering the phase right after Meryl's ex-husband had just left the state when Jack used to punch himself—hard, on the side of his head—anytime we asked him to brush his teeth or put on pants.

"It's ten miles," said Paulie, jumping in. "Flat ice, start to finish."

"The kid can slide and glide," said Neil. "Can't he?"

"Anybody can slide and glide," I said.

"It's just . . ." said Meryl, her face overtaken by a rush of sadness once again, so deep and fast moving, it almost looked like grief. About what, I wondered. Jack and his meltdowns? Me? Spending time with me? Us in general?

Then I got it. It was that kind of affair, when even the briefest separation makes your heart feel suctioned out of your chest. "I don't know," she said. "About a trip right now."

I pinched out a candle, stared at the smoke black on my fingers. The silence festered and spread down the table. Janice looked at Neil, who looked at Paulie, who looked at me. "Jack will be fine," he said. "You guys should go ahead."

. . .

Ending up the least successful of all your friends does have its advantages. Paulie lent us his sat phone. Neil offered to fly us out in his Beaver. Ginny dropped off a high-tech snowsuit for a ten-year-old that worked in temps down to forty below. It was purple, but a version that Jack would call "girl purple." She held it out to me. She had a soft, round look that people mistook for plumpness until they saw her swing an eighty-pound pack onto her back. "Meryl was right," I said. "Jack will quit. And bite. He'll lie down and kick off his skis."

"Where is Meryl?" said Ginny.

I shrugged. "Showing a house?"

"Bobby," she said. "Can't you get a job?"

"I have one," I said. "Almost." The job was a freelance gig designing brochures for the state tourist board. I was supposed to follow up with a conference call on Monday, which wasn't going to happen while we were eight hundred miles away from civilization.

"There's something you need to know," she said. "But don't get mad at me."

Panic zipped down my spine, my mouth went dry. How was finding out who Meryl was fucking—in love with, whatever she was doing—going to help me now? I started picking through all the gear on the floor of the garage, the sleeping bag pads, the camp stove. Ginny got a funny look on her face. "Ten miles is just too far," she said. "That's all I meant."

"We're going—"

"I know you're going—"

"Then help me."

She picked up the camp stove, fiddled with the latch. "Jelly beans," she said, finally. "Give Jack a handful every few clicks. The sugar high will keep him from whining—at least for a while."

"I saw you as a purist. Trail mix without the chocolate chips."

She smiled—but her voice caught and, for a minute, I thought she might cry. "I have teenagers," she said. "Montessori and wooden toys are a long, long way behind me."

I thought for a minute what Meryl had been like before we'd had Conner, back when she used to send Jack to his dad's for the weekend and we stayed up all night drinking red wine and singing TV theme songs I picked out on the banjo. Her favorite was *Laverne & Shirley*, followed by *Hawaii Five-O*. I loved the way she danced with her back to me, and the secret blonde streaks that seemed to show up only when she was sleeping. When she laughed, it felt like tiny jingle bells breaking out all over my skin.

I had thought I could make her laugh like that all the time—and maybe she had thought it too. Now she was stuck paying our mortgage and pleading with Jack's principal and hauling Conner to day care so that I would have time to send out my resume and get a job with health care for Jack's therapy. We were in a credit-card free fall, not to mention Neil and the five grand he lent us last spring.

And yet, the day of the dinner party had not been unlike many other days this winter. I had spent my resume-sending time defrosting moose sausage for the jambalaya, then cruising over to Kincaid to skate-ski the long loop. Just past the halfway point, a group of high school kids whizzed past me at speeds so effortless and supernatural it seemed a little disconcerting later to find some of them just standing around like regular human beings behind a tree. They motioned me over, held out what appeared to be an e-joint. I improvised an inhale, clumsily, wishing for my old wooden one-hitter back at home and reserved only, as I had promised Meryl, for weekends.

The kids were, without exception, boys. Boys in snowflake hats and skinny too-long bodies, flushed with sweat and heat, smelling faintly, underneath the perfumed vapor, of just-eaten oranges. I wasn't joking when I told them that I wanted my boys to grow up and be like them when they were older.

They laughed, not unkindly. Then warned me that two hits got you pretty loaded.

It had been a long day, a longer year. I did five.

Just for the record: Though Ginny had said that jelly beans were cheaper than power gels and did not melt in your pocket, Meryl was never, ever going to let me give Jack candy. He had what the school called an environmental sensitivity problem, which the doctor and therapist said video games and refined sugar did not help. My opinion was that Jack loved his mother and did not like me, and this was not such a problem, as long as we weren't out in the wilderness, on a trip that I had come up with to save our marriage while high on Matanuska Thunder Fuck, grown from "choice heirloom seed."

I groaned—out loud, a real live groan, the first of my midlife life.

Ginny didn't seem to notice. "Do you remember when we used to sit around and talk about ourselves?" she said. "There were whole decades where I considered myself pretty interesting: how I felt about things, who I wanted to be."

It takes a certain kind of strength not to look down at a bottomless fissure in the frozen earth.

"All I talked about was girls," I said. "Women, I mean. How to get them to like me."

"Love," she smiled, still a little sad. "I remember that too."

As she slid on her coat, I noticed her scar. She had fallen into a crevasse a few years ago and bashed against an ice formation on the way down, ripping open her arm wrist to elbow, right through her jacket. Paulie had eventually managed to haul her out, but there had been a while when she had hung in the void by her harness, listening to the blood drizzle out of her.

It takes a certain kind of strength not to look down at a bottomless fissure in the frozen earth. Ginny, Paulie said, had looked up the whole time, up to where he and the girls were calling to her, waiting for the rope to move, waiting for them to save her. I didn't know what this meant exactly, except that, if I tried, maybe I could get Meryl to feel the same way about me.

• • •

An hour before our 4:00 AM start, I woke up with a dreamy feeling that had something to do with Ginny and Meryl and the snow that had been falling as I skied back to my car, so high that flakes felt like soft, quiet pieces of cloud.

To my surprise, Meryl was already awake. She was staring at the ceiling. "Did you ever run away?" she said. "You know, as a kid?"

"Jack's not going to run away," I said. "But he might set fire to the house."

"I ran away," she said. "My idea of running away was to go out to the garage and sit there miserable, smoking my mother's menthols."

> "Jack's not going to run away," I said. "But he might set fire to the house."

I waited for a minute, understanding that under no circumstance should I say I ran away all the time, or that running away was fun—right up until the point it suddenly wasn't. The way a trip to the dentist was until he stopped letting you play with the model jaw and whipped out the drill. I rolled over to face her. I went right into a story, the old winsome kind I used to ply her with on dates. I did not know where it was going; it was a memory, how back when I was a kid—maybe six, maybe seven—all the happiness in the world could be found at JCPenney.

This was back in the 1970s. My dad, like all the dads in the neighborhood, worked six weeks on, six weeks off on the slope for the pipeline. By week five of his being gone, my sister and I were fighting over ownership of the crack in the couch. Desperate, exhausted, Mom would drive us all downtown, where the retail options in Anchorage at the time consisted mostly of Nude Model Studios and Arctic Fur Showrooms.

And yet, there stood JCPenney—a glamorous land of discount gold and slip-and-slide linoleum. Once past the handbags, my sister looked at me. And I looked at her. And we broke free, leaving Mom trying on Isotoner gloves at a counter. There were games we played in the vast, rambling store—hiding toasters in the dryers in Appliances, stealing credit-card carbons from the trash cans.

On the day we split up, we'd had some kind of argument. My sister flounced off. Though I wanted to follow her, I remained in Modern Fashions. For a while I did the usual—spinning a rack of blouses until they blurred into a gauzy polyester fog. But alone, nothing felt the same. The store grew vaster and shinier and more professional. I stuck my thumb in my mouth and slipped inside a rack of pants.

The pants were wool, impenetrable. Overhead, the glass circle on the rack funneled down a dusty beam of light. A broken hanger poked out from a corner. It was thick and clear with a diamond pattern cut into the plastic. When I held it up, little slivered reflections jitterbugged all over the darkness—a blizzard of tiny, electric flickers.

Hours passed or years or minutes, I couldn't tell which.

"Hours?" said Meryl, out of nowhwere, but right there beside me in the bed. "Your poor mother."

"Yeah," I said. The alarm went off on my phone—a musical meltdown of electronic glockenspiel. There was no way really to ignore it.

. . .

Port Alsworth is only a few fishing lodges, a church, and a school. In the summer, commercial hangar hands show up when a plane sets down on the landing strip, plus the occasional guide looking for new clients. That morning, that early, there was nobody. Nothing. Not even a dog. Neil helped us dump our stuff by the side of the Beaver and took off. He had a meeting back in town with his twin girls' Suzuki violin teacher.

I looked at the pile of gear, and the sharp low mountains ghosting up behind us—pale as chunks of moon and as pocked as the moon too by patches of rock. The air smelled of fuel and gravel from the village pit. The thermometer on the hangar read fifteen below and I could only hope that Meryl didn't see it.

A few lights glowed in the half dark through the trees. My plan was to hustle us away from the idea of heat and the advice of our fellow man, and hit the ice as fast as we could. Meryl and I made three trips from the runway to the dock, carrying the skis and packs, the sled, and Conner, who bounced on my shoulders, the crotch of his diaper so snug around my neck, I almost wished for a hot, cozy poop to fill it up. Except that I would have to strip off my gloves to change him.

By the time I came back, Jack had sat down on somebody's snow machine by the side of the runway. He lifted up his arms, as if for me to pick him up too, and I was tempted to, just to save the daylight that a fight would cost us. Then I shook my head. I started back with the last load. "Follow the trail,"

I said, immediately realizing this was an unfortunate move, because the first thing Jack did was wander off the trail on purpose and get stuck in a drift—the deep, heavy kind that built up over a winter of consistent snowloads one on top of another. His thrashing did not help. I dug as fast as I could. He started crying, mad-crying from what I could see through the yellow plastic of his goggles. "Mittens are for babies," he said as soon as he was out.

I sighed. I thought of the stickers in my pack—two skateboarder guys, one army helicopter—that I had brought along to slap on the snowsuit when he had a fit over the girl purple. But, as so often happens, Jack had found the one thing I had no plan for. He wanted gloves with fingers all of a sudden. He wanted my gloves. And when I explained how mittens kept your hands warmer, how my gloves were too big for him, he wanted to go home. "I miss Blackie," he said—with a cheap, victorious smile.

Just for the record: Jack had not liked Blackie. Blackie jumped on him. Blackie crapped on his pillow. That was why I had to give Blackie away before we even got him paper-trained.

And right now was when, at any other time in our lives, my voice would go tight and flat, and I would tell Jack there was no going home, home was a ninety-minute flight away through Lake Clark Pass or a ten-day hike over every kind of uncrossable mountain during which he would bite it on the first ascent. Only to have Meryl come up, give me an angry stare, and say to me, "Maybe this is too much, maybe we *should* go home." Or say to him, gently, "You're just going to have to listen to Bobby, honey. Say your anger mantra. Don't give in to fear and rage."

Which would inspire Jack to start with the terrible grunting noises that he had taken up after punching himself on the side of his head had lost its appeal—those huffing, chuffing, ragged noises that felt as if he were taking a cheese grater to your soul and just shredding, shredding off the humanity. A sound made all the more unbearable when you wondered, as I had over and over, if those ragged animal sounds might just be Jack's way of saying what he knew was true, but was too young to have the vocabulary to express: I had made love to his mother in the staff-only parking lot behind his day care. I was why his toddler car seat had been unbuckled and knocked to the floor. I was why his mother was always late to pick him up, and why his father had blown off child support. I was the dark mushroom in his little seven-year-old life, the black mold in his mind, spreading out.

But not today. Today, I reached into my inside pocket and handed him a wad of gummy worms. His eyes went big and blinky. He looked down at the brightly colored tangle glistening jewel-like in the center of his palm. "Eat it before it freezes," I said.

He nodded, too stunned to argue.

I headed down to the ice, listening for the swish-swish-swish of his snowsuit to make sure that he was following. At the dock, I strapped Conner onto the saucer, wedged a sleeping bag behind him as a backrest, held them both in place with double bungee cords. I took off my snow boots, put on my ski boots. Quickly.

Meryl had her skis on already. "Toe," she said to Jack. "Toe."

I bent down and jammed his boot tip into the binding and set it. I stood back up, I lifted his face mask and stuck a hunk of Kit Kat between his lips. Little Roman candles went off in his eyes. He giggled. I put a finger over my mouth. "Don't tell your mother," I said.

We did a pinkie promise with our thumbs, due to his mittens. Then we kicked off, shuffling across the tiny bay that led to the big open stretch of Lake Clark. It was hard, hot work, the heat gusting up from the neck of my jacket, the sweat freezing any place it was exposed to air. As we rounded past the ranger cabins and turned a hard left away from the national park, the

I had made love to his mother in the staff-only parking lot behind his day care.

sun broke through—the whole world a dazzle of ice and blue and light.

We caught a rhythm, all of us: slide, glide, slide, glide, Meryl in the lead, me bringing up the rear, slowed by the sled. The air tasted the way it does only in deep winter, each breath a sharp mineral shock of oxygen.

Every half hour or so we stopped for water, and Meryl brought out a granola bar, beef jerky, raisins. I would watch her fuss these into both boys' mouths then, while she was busy checking Conner's diaper or mittens, I'd snap a Twix in half and watch Jack snuffle it down, his brown spit freezing in a ring around his lips. Ginny had been right about the jelly beans. Chocolate melted in your pocket. By the fourth or fifth stop, I had chocolate on my gloves, Jack had chocolate in his hair. We tried to wipe it off, but Meryl caught us.

Before she could yell, I stuffed a drippy hunk of Butterfinger in her mouth.

"This is—" she said, chewing, "not even food."

"It's a candy bar," said Jack, in a tone usually reserved for introducing God.

She looked at him and me—then surrendered, saying only, "Don't let Conner see, okay?" At the next break, I handed her a handful of Goobers and that was that. She'd always loved movie candy.

· · ·

By the time we passed Mitch Cartwright's island, we were flying. Mitch Cartwright had brought the first cell phone service to Alaska and spent the weekends out here in the summer. The snow had flattened all the willows and alders around his private runway, allowing us to see the whole log spectacle from the ice: the houses and guesthouses and the barns, the long narrow building that I had heard had a lap pool inside, filled with heated glacial water. Smoke drifted out from the caretaker's chimney.

I was there with my family, the world a white crackled eggshell with us in the cup of it.

From out of nowhere, a black horse came blowing down the length of the island like a piece of living cinder, his breath trailing white behind him.

He stopped. He reared up and pawed the air and screamed.

It was magnificent. And not quite real. And I was glad I hadn't seen it alone—with the ice creaking underneath us, stretching so far in the distance, you understood why explorers believed there might just be an edge to the earth. I looked at Meryl and she smiled and squeezed my arm, Jack standing beside her, his eyes round as planets under his goggles.

Village rumor had it that Mitch was turning this part of the country into a suburb, that soon the lake and shore would look like Anchorage—and maybe those rumors were true. But for once, I was not torn up about it. I was not thinking how I hadn't ended up like Mitch, or even Neil; how I didn't own even a cabin and still had to rent us one from the old Dena'ina family who owned most of the far shoreline. I was too busy watching Jack study his bootlace with the kind of wonder that laces have when you don't know how to tie them, while Meryl inched up the mask on Conner's sleeping face, so tenderly that a memory of my own mother floated through me—the way she used to brush her fingers over the back of my neck when she passed by me doing homework at the dining room table. And at that moment, I didn't want my own cabin. I didn't want anything—or to be anywhere else. I was there with my family, the world a white crackled egg-shell with us in the cup of it.

Then Jack pitched a snowball at my back and I threw one at him. At that moment, as so often happens in Alaska, the clouds should have swept in and a blizzard set in. Only they didn't. The sun kept on, gilding the mountains at the edges, softening the snow under our skis. We went for a few more clicks, singing "The Wheels on the Bus" for Conner and "Yellow Submarine" for Jack. An hour or so later, we arrived at the beach with daylight to spare.

We kicked out of our skis and headed up. From the beach to the cabin was no more than fifty feet, but with the deep snow you couldn't tell what was path or alders. Finally, I ended up breaking a trail alone, using my body weight and a lot of struggling and stamping. All the windows and doors on the deck were boarded up with plywood and bear nails sticking pointed end out. The hammer I had left in the plastic tub under the eave was still there, and I started clawing off the nails that held the plywood over the doorframe. Jack came up behind me. "I could help," he said.

"Sure you could," I said, trying to think of something he could do without bashing open a thumb.

Meryl struggled up the stairs, Conner in her arms. He was crying. "Didn't you hear us?" she said.

"I heard you," Jack said.

"Me too," I said—but not as believably.

Jack and I stood up a little straighter. Meryl lifted Conner up on her hip. "He won't take water, he's not cold. What if he's got a fever?" I stripped off my glove liners and felt his forehead, which felt warm, but we all were warm, we had been busting hump for six hours.

"Maybe he's mad," said Jack.

"About what?" snapped Meryl. She began to pace around. Conner's crying built, insistent, and getting stronger, then weaker, then stronger again. The sweat on my neck grew clammy. The light was fading, the temperature dropping. I began to get tense; we all did. Conner never cried. He was the kind of kid who just scooted around, pulling things off the table and laughing when they boinked on the floor. I started ripping at the nails around the edges of plywood, trying to remember if nailheads broke off at twenty below or not. "Stand back," I said to Jack, more sharply than I'd planned.

He looked slapped. Conner wailed, harder and harder. "Jack," I said. "Jack, I'm sorry." I reached into my pocket. The chocolate was gone, and we were down to the sack of jelly beans. I held out a handful. He shrugged—done with sugar, apparently.

"Just get the door open," said Meryl. "I think I have a thermometer in the pack."

"I'm trying," I said.

"You said I could help," said Jack. "I can hold the hammer." I gave a terrific pull and the bear door came crashing down, a few nails flying, exposing the other door, the beat-up one that dated back to the guy in the 1950s who had built the place for trapping. We stumbled inside. The room was dark, the table and the stove frosted over. I threw kindling, starter, logs into the stove, moving faster and faster as Conner cried and raged and cried. Meryl tried to give him a raisin. No. No. No. Which with his lisp came out sounding like Wo. Wo. Wo. Though perhaps that was what he was trying to express. Some kind of existential toddler despair.

"What's wrong with him?" she said.

"How should I know?" I said. But I checked his nose for frostbite—none—then pulled on a head lamp and went back for the packs, Jack following behind me in the narrow cone of light. By the time we were all inside, the stove had taken hold. And Meryl had fired up the lantern and put a pot of snow on the stove to melt. Conner was lying on the floor now, sobbing and kicking his feet.

There was nothing we could do but step around him. It was as if his crying had set loose little rats in our brains, the kind that scrabble around, chewing off the end of your thoughts. Jack began to suck his thumb. Meryl kept finding and losing the same potholder. I grabbed a canned chicken in the pantry and dumped it into the pot of melted snow with a bouillon cube and some carrots we had packed in. A layer of gray fat scum pooled along the surface, but the smell velveted through the room—salty and rich.

I stabbed a chunk of meat with a fork, held it under Conner's nose. He sat up, opened his mouth—and sucked it down, still gulping. He took another and another. The quiet that followed was golden harp music. "You did it," said Meryl, all the love in her voice suddenly back again.

I wanted to feel victorious, but couldn't find the energy. My body was falling down ahead of my mind.

The cabin was basically a low room with a slanted ceiling and a loft at one end. To reach the loft, you had to climb an eight-foot ladder. Conner couldn't sleep up there without falling down the ladder or through the hole in the floor where the ladder rested. Jack refused to spend the night in a dark, spooky corner all alone. The four of us collapsed in the big bed together.

Two hours later, I woke up and felt Meryl's hand on me. My mind was slow and clumsy with dreaming, but I felt the warmth of her fingers, her heat. Things moved so quickly, I was already out of my boxers and had her silk long underwear down around her feet. The kids were sleeping like kittens on either side of us. I shifted with my hip, right up behind her—and I could have just slid in. I almost did. The feel of her narrow back, her liquid white skin, still ran up against the black horse and that dazzled look that had passed between us as the most perfect moment I'd had in my life.

Jack sat up. "I can't sleep," he said. "Can you sleep?"

"Yes," I said. "I'm sleeping great." I patted the bed, for him to put his head back down, but with the kind of dark urgency that always makes dogs and kids do the opposite of what you ask. He leaned over me. Meryl went rigid. Conner sighed and began fingering her breast—the way sometimes he does, as if still nursing in his dreams. I lay there. I tried not to feel my stiffness, the little hot cleft of wetness I was already half nudged into.

> **It was as if his crying had set loose little rats in our brains.**

I wriggled back into my boxers and sat up. I grabbed two sleeping bags, busted up the ladder, and went back for Jack. He didn't want to go. "Fine," I said. "I'll take Conner." On the ride up, Conner stretched awake. He seemed to think the loft was pretty awesome and began to run like a drunk firecracker from one end to other, laughing. "Come on up, Jack," I said. "I can't come down."

"Bobby," said Meryl, "let's not do this."

But to my surprise, Jack poked his head through the ladder hole. I was lying with Conner on the sleeping bags. "I like ladders," he said. "You could get me a ladder at our house."

"I could!" I said. "Nobody move." I shot down and grabbed a glass of water, a pillow. And my jacket with the bag of jelly beans still in the pocket. I climbed back up the ladder. By now both boys were fully awake and Jack had to pee. Conner and I drank the water. Jack whizzed in the glass, splashing only a little. "Don't eat yellow snow," he told me.

"Don't drink yellow water," I said. Then I told him slowly, calmly, that I needed him to do a big responsible job. He had to cuddle up with his little brother for five minutes. I would time him. He could not, under any circumstances, let his brother near the ladder hole. "You said you wanted to help," I said. I held up the bag of jelly beans. "You can eat them all," I said. "The whole time I'm gone—and then I'll be back."

"Okay," he said. He took the bag. He dumped it onto the floor and began moving the pieces of candy around like little cars or robots, making scarily accurate machine-gun noises. This was the kind of game Conner loved, one that let him sit and worship his brother with his eyes, saying in his lispy voice, "My turn now, Wack? My turn?"

> I think what I was supposed to do was go down and ask Meryl if she had enjoyed fucking Paulie.

I climbed back down, skipping the last two rungs. All we had was five minutes. All we needed was five minutes. Meryl was on her side, her face not alive with desire, but not set against me either. My woody was gone. I spit into my hand and brought it back to life. I leaned behind her. I kissed her on the back of her neck, her shoulders, and all the way down the way she liked— and for a minute she rubbed against me, her ass wiggling into me, and we were there, I was there. Until I pushed myself up on my elbow and caught her hair and somehow yanked it across the bed when I slipped.

"Ouch," she said. "Jesus. Can't you just stop?"

The expression on her face. I took a minute, the kind of minute you need to take when you realize you are feeling one thing and the other person is feeling something so very, very different than you are—despite that other person's body beside you.

"Mommy?" said Conner. He was at the hole. I leapt out of bed and up the ladder and led him back the corner and his sleeping bag. Jack was flicking the jelly beans across the room as if they were marbles.

"You were supposed to watch Conner," I said.

"I was," said Jack.

I hunched low and made my way over. A jelly bean hit my foot. It was a red one. It tasted like all jelly beans—a mouthful of sugar sawdust. I ate another and lay down. Conner came over and tried to sit on my chest. His diaper was wet.

"Here," I said. "Try one."

He made his wrinkle face.

"No, not the green," I said. "Try a red. All the cool kids eat red."

Another wrinkle face.

"He's sick of jelly beans," said Jack—in an absent-minded way, still working on how to flick one bean into another with enough force to spin it across the floor. "Uncle Paulie gave him the whole bag last time and he ate all the black ones and threw up."

I stopped—all of me, my heart, my body. So did Jack. He looked at me. It was dark in the loft and hard to see the fine details of another person's face, but I knew the expression. His mouth was working around, trying to find a way to unsay what he'd said. "Uncle Paulie sure eats a lot of jelly beans," I said, in a casual stepdad voice, nonchalant.

Jack's face collapsed.

"It's okay," I said. "It'll all be okay."

He whispered, "Does this mean we don't get the Xbox?"

Somewhere under my skin, my face looked like his. When he lay down on the sleeping bag in a tight little ball, weeping so quietly, so profoundly, I hoped that his grief really was about the Xbox and not everything else that he probably, somehow, had figured out.

Conner went over to him and started patting his head. "Don't be wad, Wack. Don't be wad."

I felt very strange. I think what I was supposed to do was go down and ask Meryl if she had enjoyed fucking Paulie while our kids ate Ginny's candy and played her teenager daughter's video games. But the loft wasn't soundproof. She had probably heard us already. I heard a shuffling sound, as if she were packing or just picking stuff up and putting it down, not knowing what to do. Jack had his face in his hands.

"Everybody messes up," I said. My voice was breaking, but I knew better than to stop talking. "Do you want to hear about the time that I messed up?"

He nodded.

And I told him about me hiding inside the rack of pants at JCPenney, as if it were a cozy bedtime story. I told him how the salesladies and store detectives were searching the store for me, and how I didn't hear them and didn't notice and didn't come out. Until my mom found me. Because moms knew where you were. They could smell you.

"Did you lose all your privileges?" Jack said, Conner already passed out beside him.

"Yes," I said. "I lost all my privileges."

And with that, the sobbing began—silent and racking, my only noise a ragged intake of breath. Jack still had his face in his hands, I could not see if he heard me or if he'd fallen asleep. As I made my way to the ladder, I thought of the grown-up part of the story I had omitted for him, though maybe I shouldn't have. Maybe he was the one person who might have understood it.

My mother had been a young mother at the time, and when she raked open the hangers on the rack, I saw her face and shrank back—ready for a yell, a panicked slap. But she paused. Her face softened, and she stepped inside and sat down across from me, cross-legged in the darkness. Neither of us spoke. The quiet was the quiet of children alone with a toy they don't mind sharing and I was surprised she knew not to ruin it.

I smiled, then held up the crystal hanger and made the little flickering lights bounce off the dark. She gasped with delight—the real kind that almost sounds like fear.

Outside, the salespeople and detectives were still calling my name. I could hear them now. She could hear them too, but we stayed there together, my mother with a finger over her lips until I knew, the way you know about grown-ups when you are little, even if they won't tell you, that she didn't want to leave either. Not now, not ever. Not to go back to our car or our street or our house. And I felt rich and special to know this— that my mother was unhappy, even if I didn't know why and couldn't fix it.

It was only when we heard my sister's voice calling, and my mother didn't move and didn't move, that I began to get scared. My sister sounded as if she were crying. My mother smiled at me, her face white, smooth, almost serene. "Bobby!" my sister was calling, "Bobby!"

I looked at my mother. I took her hand—and led us out.

I was six years old at the time, maybe seven. I was forty-nine now, but with the same helpless feeling deadening through my body. Meryl was pacing below. I was standing on the ladder. I waited, listening, as if there were anywhere else to go but down. 🛡

Gerardo Pacheco Matus

A HEAP OF ASHES

this is the story of how my mother
turned into a heap of ashes

mother was in charge of fetching water
for the pig slaughter

the big metal cauldron was as shiny as a nickel

my father wasn't around as much
grandmother said   my father drowned
his pain with lots of mescal

my siblings rested in the middle of the fields
buried at the foot of the giant lime tree

piglets born every day like weeds
the old butcher was as strong as a horse

mother was the most beautiful
& happy woman on this earth
when father didn't beat her

this is a story of slapping   punching
kicking   crying & burnt meat

SHOE BOX COFFIN

my brothers lay
inside a tiny coffin
a cardboard shoe box
father had spared
from the fire

my brothers breathed
with such difficulty
their lips & skin had turned
purple like a drowned fish

mother sobbed in her hammock
as the old midwife had lost
another battle against death

the old midwife's shaky hands
had cut the umbilical cord
that joined mother & the dead

the old midwife placed
my brothers' corpses
with such care facing each other
inside the shoe box

she covered the tiny coffin
with her old rebozo
before she left to never come back

my sisters lit white candles
around the shoe box
a cloud of rue & camphor
swallowed their hard faces

the wind entered the house
to lick our feet with its wet tongue
& the tamarind trees fell
to the ground with loud thuds

the night arrived sad & dark
perfect for ghost stories
but no one wanted to listen
about the dead

THE BURNING

grandmother knew my father
was el diablo   he was too drunk
to even know why he beat mother

dios bendito   grandmother said
as the devil peered through his eyes

she made the sign of the cross only once
before my father turned into el diablo

my father had an evil smile   a sneer
like a hungry dog
ready to jump onto its prey

my father entered the house with a kick
the door split unevenly   the house shook
the beams rattled & the mud walls
crumbled like sugar skulls

father didn't give mother a warning
grandmother said   he just began punching
& kicking her like he did
when the pigs fought him back

mother didn't have time to react
as she sat next to the fire making tortillas

father pushed mother into the fire
mother fell into the fire hands first
her tiny hands burnt   she screamed
so loudly   grandmother grew afraid

my dead brothers might wake up
& come back to the house
to find mother's charred bones

Rosebud Ben-Oni

POET WRESTLING WITH STARHORSE
IN THE DARK

But I am human & need to be loved just like ::

Shut your mouth & drive. Isn't that your space-

      ship parked outside ($^{\text{take me higher}}$)? How soon is

            —swept—

        leg & sing   tumbling

           down Queens

Boulevard of eight lanes I

      know better ($^{\text{the wrong way}}$ just like

        everybody—)

& left it on the ground today,

     this mass of mine seeping

       & numbness & my neurologist won't curse you

rabid skateboard

    won't name you

        coward
                when under floodlight examination

           :: you do not appear ::

        loyal & grieved.
                My love is—

another thing.

He does not believe in you & listens

            for you in the dark. Never asks for proof

                        I cannot give him.
                      It's hard to speak plainly
                   when they ask what you are.
               They assume I am still all human

(need to be)

                    & not a war

      (loved)

            between the two.

            That to become
            yours is to lose

now that I write of our alien love in the dark.

     No metaphors,
         no closet doors,
             when I say

     I read love poems to an alien in the dark
        & demand ($^{\text{how soon is}}$) embrace.

                    ,

  Your kind does not do such things.
     & sometimes it's tempting,
       to be a kind of new
         to the universe.

                                        But I am human
                                      because I need
                                        home & home
                                    is giving each other
                                our blood & our bones & you
                                        have neither
                            dearest wandering flash & fire —

Farewell. Best
wishes & kindest regards
of the fifth kind. I've already
waited too long & all my nerves are

                        centripetally yours
                            singing ::

                our starbird cry,

        oh smashmouth
                        oh cinder-
            block
                shine.

RECIPE FOR
MYSTERY

Elissa Schappell

Char-truce

There is something devilish about Chartreuse, a liqueur long associated with lawlessness and vice, being made by holy men. And something divine.

In 1605 the Carthusian monks in the village of Vauvert were gifted an ancient manuscript, a mysterious recipe for the "Elixir of Long Life." Little was known of the author, beyond the obvious: he or she was a superior alchemist with a knowledge of botany and a skill for distillation that far exceeded that of the monastery's apothecaries. At the beginning of the

eighteenth century, the document was passed along to La Grande Chartreuse monastery to decipher, a task that took nearly a century.

Chartreuse as we know it is the coalescence of 130 herbs, botanicals, and spices. No one is certain exactly what the ingredients are, or what esoteric processes the monks employ to create their enigmatic liqueur. The monks are just as secretive today as they were hundreds of years ago. To protect the sanctity of the recipe, only two monks possess the necessary knowledge at any given time: one charged with gathering the various plants, flowers, and spices, the other with the maceration and blending of the elements.

What does Chartreuse taste like? It's almost impossible to compare it to another drink. Chartreuse isn't *like* anything else in the same way that the ocean isn't like anything else. You could say Chartreuse is like Galliano because it's made of herbs and spices, but that's like saying the ocean is like a lake because it's made of water.

When I am asked I say, *Imagine a deep green meadow. Now imagine it on fire.*

· · ·

I don't remember the first time I tasted Chartreuse, only that it was from my father's glass.

· · ·

The Lord works in mysterious ways. The fact that Chartreuse exists at all is a testament to faith and devotion, as well as the rebel spirit of the brotherhood. Twice, during an anticlerical purge and later in a government takeover of the distillery, the monks were expelled from France. The first time, during the French Revolution, the monk who possessed the formula was arrested with it still hidden on his person. Had he not managed to smuggle it out of jail, the recipe would have been lost. Had Frère Jérôme Maubec, a newly installed apothecary, failed to reach the deathbed of the old apothecary, had the dying man

been too infirm to pass along what he had gleaned, Frère Jérôme would not, in 1737, have succeeded in producing the elusive Elixir of Long Life. Had the monks not thought to bottle and sell the brew via mule in the local village, and had the villagers not become hooked on the herbaceous, highly alcoholic, and mildly hallucinogenic "health tonic" (69 percent alcohol, 138 proof), there would have been no reason to keep producing the elixir, or, in 1764, refine it into the intensely pleasurable liqueur they'd name Green Chartreuse (55 percent alcohol, 110 proof). Had the monks decided not to return from exile in Spain in 1921 (they'd fled France in the second anticlerical purge and while in exile made a Spanish version of Chartreuse), and had they not returned to the distillery and taken up production again, it would have been a crime.

No. It would have been a sin.

· · ·

Evelyn Waugh, despite being a fool for the stuff, wasn't fool enough to take a stab at describing its taste, yet he manages in *Brideshead Revisited* to capture Chartreuse's *je ne sais quoi* by having the flamboyant, stuttering Anthony Blanche describe it thusly: "There are five distinct tastes as it trickles over the tongue. It is like swallowing a sp-spectrum."

I like that Waugh didn't know what is in Chartreuse, and neither will I.

In that not knowing, we are free to imagine the botanical spectrum. And in imagining all the possible grasses, flowers, herbs, spices, and roots, the world expands.

• • •

Grasses: blades of bright green grass, spiky blue-green grass, knee-high grasses that shush with the wind, tall yellow grasses that explode out of the ground, feathery grasses that mass in clumps, wavy tasseled grasses, shy grasses that grow between rocks, grasses that riot across hillsides.

• • •

The Carthusians are renowned for being one of the strictest and most cloistered orders in Christendom. Their vows stress not only poverty, obedience, and celibacy but also silence. They shun all society, including family, in favor of "the vocation of solitude." They are entirely self-sufficient. When they are not in their cells in prayer and contemplation, they are growing and cooking their own food, chopping wood to feed the furnaces in winter, and making pottery. They do not leave the monastery save for once a week when the brothers enjoy a long restorative hike. During this time they may speak. On a quiet day you can hear them singing Gregorian chants to the trees.

On the Carthusians' official website they reassure readers concerned about the deleterious effects of such extreme

isolation. "The love of God," they assure us, is "inebriating."

• • •

The majority of times that I have felt the most alive, the most awake, the most certain of my purpose, have been in the act of writing. When I am, as someone once said, *praying words together*.

When I am writing well I forget I have a body.

• • •

Flowers: purple flowers in bud, yellow blossoms freckled orange, tiny pink flowers that bloom upside down, red flowers with starburst-shaped pistils, flowers the color of winter at night, trumpet flowers that snake on a vine, flowers with heads crusted with pollen, shy flowers that close when you touch them, flowers with petals that feel just like skin.

• • •

The recipes for Green Chartreuse, which is aged two to three years, and the V.E.P. Chartreuse, which is aged upward of ten, have remained unchanged since 1764. In 1838 the Carthusians added Yellow Chartreuse, a sweeter, mellower, less alcoholic (only 40 percent alcohol, 80 proof) version, which gets its sunny good looks from an infusion of saffron.

Imagine a deep green meadow. Now imagine it on fire.

The monks continue to produce Élixir Végétal de la Grande-Chartreuse—Chartreuse in its earliest incarnation. Unfortunately, because *technically* it is still considered an herbal medicine (it is, after all, called the Elixir of Long Life) and thus subject to annoying FDA regulations, it's not distributed in the United States.

Which is not to say, were you to go to Europe and buy a small bottle or twelve and bring them to me, that you or I would get into any trouble.

But trouble does seem to follow Chartreuse.

The holy father of gonzo journalism, Hunter S. Thompson, had a demon's thirst for the stuff, considering it essential to his creative process, along with Chivas, cigarettes, and cocaine. Tom Waits growls its praises in "Til the Money Runs Out." Short of a Roman candle, Fitzgerald could not signal Gatsby's glamorous degeneracy better than having Gatsby ply Nick and Daisy with Chartreuse he's "taken from a cupboard in the wall." The minute Nick's lips touch the lip of that glass, his fate is sealed and any chance of leaving East Egg with his innocence intact is gone.

. . .

For as long as my father was alive he bought my Chartreuse. My mother buys it for me now. You could say it is our family's drink.

> When I break the wax on the neck of the bottle, I dare pretend a monk has personally made it for me.

We prefer the V.E.P. While it is harder to find, only a limited amount produced every year, it's less sweet and syrupy than the standard Chartreuse, which is better suited to cocktails. The V.E.P. is a different kind of burn. Because Chartreuse is the rare liqueur whose flavor improves with time in the bottle, the vintage is important.

You can determine the vintage by looking at the label on the back of the bottle, where you will find a series of numbers. Add the first three digits of this number to 1084, the year the order was founded, and voilà.

Compounding the pleasure, the V.E.P. bottle is a replicate of the original. It is corked by hand and sealed with wax, stamped with a wax seal on the back, and shipped in a special wooden box, marked with a branding iron, that looks like a coffin.

When I break the wax on the neck of the bottle, I dare pretend a monk has personally made it for me.

. . .

Spices: spices that are bark, spices that are buds, spices that are fruit, spices that are seeds, spices that are stigma.

. . .

It's terrible to imagine the secret recipe coming up on a Google search. I wince at the thought of the formula flashing on a computer screen, being spit out of a printer in some sterile industrial production facility in New Jersey.

I prefer to picture a monk in a white robe and rope belt, repeating the list to himself as he swings his scythe, digs up roots with a blessed trowel, hikes back to the monastery rattling a handful of seeds in his hand like dice.

• • •

Even chemists—capable of breaking the rarefied liqueur down to its cellular level—are unable to explain with any certainty how the monks conjure the spirit, or what sort of mystical transformation occurs in its distillation.

I have no patience for people who can't watch a magic trick without wanting to yank back the curtain and demand an explanation. This discomfort, this unwillingness to cede any territory to magic and mystery, suggests to me not just a poverty of imagination but a stinginess of spirit. The pleasure I take in the universe's steady refusal to yield all its secrets to humankind, despite our feeling entitled to know them, is immense.

• • •

Chartreuse's closest relative in terms of appearance, alcohol content, and degenerate charms is absinthe. But when it comes to taste they could not be more dissimilar. The licorice-and-anise flavor of absinthe is a kick in the head, as subtle as the split knickers and rouged nipples of a Moulin Rouge show girl. Chartreuse blooms in the mouth, its sweetness opening into a complex, powerfully herbal flavor that ignites with spice, then flares in the back of the throat, leaving a long warm finish.

Absinthe is a knife at your throat, Chartreuse a silk garrote.

• • •

Roots: hairy white roots, tan roots with a fibrous peel, knobby orange roots that look like old men, pale skinny roots that spiral deep into the ground, roots that are blue and fat as a finger, stubborn roots that cling to the dirt.

• • •

Both the monk and the writer are outsiders. Both live in their heads, the monk in the act of contemplation, the writer in the act of creation. Both choose lives shaped by the practice of their passion—monks, solitary in their cells, their *desert*, exist in a state of ceaseless prayer, and writers, solitary at their desks, their *hermitage*, exist in a state of flow—their devotion demanding they eschew fellowship with other human beings in order to stay present in the moment and work. Solitary and part of a community.

• • •

"The job of the artist," Francis Bacon said, "is always to deepen the mystery."

· · ·

To experience fully the majesty of Chartreuse you must master the imbiber's version of the French inhale. Do this: take a sip, hold it in your mouth, savor it, let the flavor build, don't swallow, now, on the breath, exhale the vapors, let them rise up, then breathe in through your nose.

The first time I always gasp a little. The second time it's easier. I can breathe deeper, fill myself up with the spirit, let my head fall back, and now my muscles go soft. My body hums.

· · ·

Modern scientific analysis can explain how Vermeer created the illusion of a three-dimensional space using a camera obscura but not how he captured the luminosity of natural light or the rising blush on the cheek of a young girl.

How did Jackson Pollock summon meaning and beauty out of the improvisational drips and splatterings of paint on canvas?

How did Virginia Woolf write *The Waves*? Out of all the words in the world how did she know those were the ones?

· · ·

Herbs: bitter herbs with waxy leaves, pungent herbs that grow in bristles, sour herbs with shield-shaped leaves, herbs the color of copper pennies, herbs with leaves like lacy fans, exotic herbs that wilt on picking, sticky herbs with corkscrew stems, herbs with leaves that look dipped in wine, herbs with pin-sized flowers that float like confetti.

· · ·

With only the vaguest signposts, guided by inspiration and operating on faith and instinct, the monks created in Chartreuse a masterpiece that does what Allen Ginsberg believed poetic language does as well: it connects heaven and earth.

Why, when I drink it, do I think: *This is mine. This belongs to me. This is mine.*

I feel this way about very few things. I do not know. I cannot tell you. I have only signposts. Grass. Flower. Herb. Spice. Root. 🜍

Joshua James Amberson lives in a basement in Portland, Oregon. He's currently working on a book about eyeballs.

Sally Ball is the author of *Wreck Me* and *Annus Mirabilis*. She teaches at ASU and is associate director of Four Way Books.

Mildred Barya teaches creative writing at UNC-Asheville. She has published three poetry books and is a board member of African Writers Trust.

Rosebud Ben-Oni is a 2014 NYFA Fellow and a CantoMundo Fellow; her collection, *turn around, BRXGHT XYXS* is forthcoming in 2019.

Tabitha Blankenbiller lives outside of Portland, Oregon. Her work has appeared in numerous publications, and her essay collection, *Eats of Eden*, is now available.

Ruby Brunton is a New Zealand-raised writer who lives between Brooklyn and Mexico City. She's had essays in *Hazlitt*, the *New Inquiry*, and *Hyperallergic*.

Adam Clay's most recent book is *Stranger*. He teaches at the University of Southern Mississippi and edits *Mississippi Review*.

Carrie Grinstead lives in Los Angeles with her partner, Daniel, and Pickle, their rat terrier. She works as a hospital librarian.

James Hoch's books are *A Parade of Hands* and *Miscreants*. Currently, he is professor of creative writing at Ramapo College of New Jersey.

Cheston Knapp is the author of *Up Up, Down Down* and the managing editor of *Tin House*.

Yusef Komunyakaa has won many awards for his poetry, including the Pulitzer Prize. He teaches at NYU.

Catherine Lacey is the author of the books *Nobody Is Ever Missing*, *The Answers*, and *Certain American States*.

Ursula K. Le Guin (1929-2018) was one of America's finest writers. Her work will continue to inspire writers and readers the world over.

Teddy Macker is the author of *This World*, a collection of poems. He lives on a small farm in Carpinteria, California.

Gerardo Pacheco Matus, a Mayan Native poet, educator, and essayist, loves to hike on the hills of California where grass and crows thrive.

Shane McCrae's next book of poetry is called *The Gilded Auction Block*. He teaches at Columbia University and lives in New York City.

Philip Metres is the author of *Sand Opera*. A two-time recipient of the NEA and the Arab American Book Award, he teaches at John Carroll University.

Jon Michaud is a novelist and librarian who lives in Maplewood, New Jersey. He is a regular contributor to the *Washington Post* and NewYorker.com.

Leigh Newman is the author of the memoir *Still Points North*.

Meghan O'Gieblyn is a writer who lives in Wisconsin. Her essay collection, *Interior States*, is forthcoming.

Abbey Mei Otis is successful and dangerous. Her story collection, *Alien Virus Love Disaster*, is forthcoming in 2018.

Lia Purpura's latest collection is *It Shouldn't Have Been Beautiful*. *All the Fierce Tethers* (essays) will be out in 2019. She teaches at UMBC.

Ira Sadoff's last book was *True Faith*; recent poems have appeared in the *New Yorker*, *APR*, and the Poem-a-Day series from the Academy of American Poets.

Elissa Schappell is a cofounder and the editor-at-large of *Tin House*, as well as a full-time murderer of great ideas.

Maggie Smith is the author of, most recently, *Good Bones* and *The Well Speaks of Its Own Poison*.

J. Jezewska Stevens is a writer and teacher living in New York. Follow her on Twitter @JezewskaJ.

Nomi Stone's second collection of poems, *Kill Class*, is forthcoming in 2019. Poems appear recently in the *New Republic* and *Best American Poetry*.

Ashley Whitaker is a writer from Texas. She received an MFA from the University of Michigan. This is her first published story.

Ashleigh Young is a poet and editor at Victoria University Press. Her first book of essays, *Can You Tolerate This?*, received Yale's Windham-Campbell Prize.

FRONT COVER:
The Secrets of the Night, watercolor and gouache on paper, 19.6″ x 25.5″, 2013 © Luisa Rivera. www.luisarivera.cl.

CREDITS:
Page 50: From *Can You Tolerate This?* by Ashleigh Young, to be published on July 3, 2018 by Riverhead Books, an imprint of Penguin Publishing Group, a division of Penguin Random House LLC. Copyright © 2018 by Ashleigh Young.

W

Abandon

VOL. XXXI NO. 1 | SPRING 2018

WITNESSMAG.ORG

Ravi Shankar says, "...Sybil is that rarest of white writers who, because she's worked so hard at it, genuinely understands a good part of what it means to be a person of color.

IMMIGRATION ESSAYS

When Baker received a MakeWork grant to write about Chattanooga's unheard voices, she had no idea that her project would take her from the homes of Chattanooga's refugees in "Landings" to what Critical Flame calls a "Sebaldian travelogue through the Syrian migration route" in "Reverse Migration." From her childhood home near Ferguson, Missouri, to her travels as an expatriate living in Asia, to the troubled cities of Eastern Europe, Baker explores the physical and emotional wanderings of what Mary McCarthy calls "exiles, expatriates, and internal emigres."

"Adventures of a Fake Immigrant" and "Schemers" examines her ambivalent complicity in Chattanooga's rapid gentrification and the erasure of its historically black neighborhoods.

Using photos, literature, and her own family's slave-owning history, Baker excavates her own past as well as Chattanooga's to try and understand the ghosts that haunt her and the city she inhabits. With a poignancy that is particularly relevant for these times, the voices in this collection echo through the text and shine brightly through the dark.

SYBIL BAKER

Nonfiction / Essays + $16.00 + CRPRESS.ORG

From *Tin House*'s Managing Editor, an exhilarating, profound collection of linked essays on becoming who you are.

"Always smart, often hilarious, and ultimately transcendent."
—ANTHONY DOERR

"Uncanny… joyously expansive."
—MAGGIE NELSON

"Full of wit and disquiet… A glittering collection."
—LESLIE JAMISON

"Exuberant… Acerbically funny…Deserves to be widely read."
—PUBLISHERS WEEKLY

"Masterful…pure delight."
—BOOKLIST

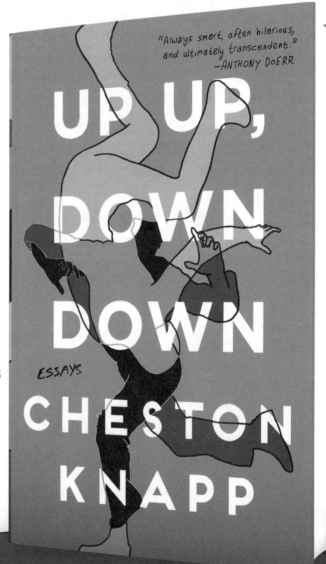

MFA
CREATIVE WRITING
FICTION – POETRY

TEXAS ★ STATE
UNIVERSITY®
The rising STAR of Texas

Our campus overlooks the scenic Hill Country town of San Marcos, part of the Austin Metropolitan Area. With Austin just 30 miles to the north, Texas State students have abundant opportunities to enjoy music, dining, outdoor recreation, and more.

Tim O'Brien
Professor of Creative Writing

Naomi Shihab Nye
Visiting Professor 2017-18

Karen Russell
Endowed Chair 2017-19

Faculty

Fiction
Doug Dorst
Jennifer duBois
Tom Grimes
Debra Monroe

Poetry
Cyrus Cassells
Roger Jones
Cecily Parks
Kathleen Peirce
Steve Wilson

Visiting Writers*
Gabrielle Calvocoressi
Lydia Davis
Junot Díaz
Stephen Dunn
Stuart Dybek
Martín Espada
Ross Gay
Jorie Graham
Lauren Groff
Terrance Hayes
Marlon James
Leslie Jamison
Adam Johnson
Ada Limón
Philipp Meyer
Mary Ruefle
Tracy K. Smith
Ocean Vuong

* Recent and upcoming

Adjunct Thesis Faculty
Lee K. Abbott
Gina Apostol
Catherine Barnett
Rick Bass
Kevin Brockmeier
Gabrielle Calvocoressi
Ron Carlson
Victoria Chang
Maxine Chernoff
Joanna Klink
Eduardo Corral
Charles D'Ambrosio
Natalie Diaz
John Dufresne
Carolyn Forché
James Galvin
Amelia Gray
Saskia Hamilton
Amy Hempel
Bret Anthony Johnston

T. Geronimo Johnson
Li-Young Lee
Karan Mahajan
Nina McConigley
Elizabeth McCracken
Jane Mead
Mihaela Moscaliuc
David Mura
Kirstin Valdez Quade
Spencer Reece
Alberto Ríos
Elissa Schappell
Richard Siken
Gerald Stern
Natalia Sylvester
Justin Torres
Brian Turner
Eleanor Wilner
Monica Youn

Now offering courses in creative nonfiction.

$70,000 Scholarship:
W. Morgan and Lou Claire Rose Fellowship for an incoming student. Additional scholarships and teaching assistantships available.

Front Porch, our literary journal:
frontporchjournal.com

Doug Dorst, MFA Director
Department of English

601 University Drive
San Marcos, TX 78666-4684
512.245.7681

MEMBER **THE TEXAS STATE UNIVERSITY SYSTEM**

Texas State University, to the extent not in conflict with federal or state law, prohibits discrimination or harassment on the basis of race, color, national origin, age, sex, religion, disability, veterans' status, sexual orientation, gender identity or expression. Texas State University is a tobacco-free campus. 16-578 6-16

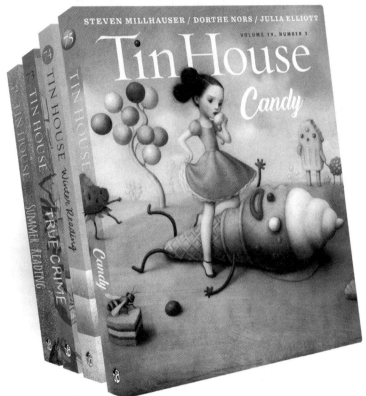

ABOUT THE COVER

This issue's cover artist, Luisa Rivera, sees a creation myth in her painting *The Secrets of the Night*. Though the women depicted are decidedly modern—Rivera says they remind her of "themed synchronized swimmers"—they speak to the ancient tradition of storytelling. The secrets they share generate "something strange that allows the earth to be shaped around them." They manifest ideas of mythology and folklore.

Nature and the female figure have always been instinctual subjects for Rivera. Now she approaches those themes with more intention and other topics have emerged for her, such as spirituality, mythology, and environmental issues. In addition to her figurative work, she has a number of pieces that play with patterns of flora and fauna, inspired by the designs of William Morris.

Rivera enjoys studying gestures, often using multiple photo references for one piece. She combines images, "like a collage: the hand from one, the nose from the other." She primarily works by hand with watercolor and gouache and makes final adjustments digitally. Rivera finds the layering of water-based paints meditative, a process in which she can trust her intuition.

Rivera's palette has a vintage quality. The composition in *The Secrets of the Night* is almost baroque in its use of diagonal shapes and movement. Her aesthetic has been called surrealist, but she identifies more with magical realism, "which creates uncanny or strange atmospheres in daily scenarios." Her lush flora and narrative style made her the perfect artist for the illustrated edition of a classic of magical realism, Gabriel Garcia Marquez's *One Hundred Years of Solitude*. You can see more of Rivera's art at www.luisarivera.cl.

Written by *Tin House* designer Jakob Vala, based on an interview with the artist.